For amanda

Hope you enjoy it. No. 2 – get ready for No 3.

with love
Sue
x

The Tears of Time

Susan Hanson

All Rights Reserved. No part of this publication may be reproduced in any form or by any means, including scanning, photocopying, or otherwise without prior written permission of the copyright holder.
(c) Copyright 2013 Susan Hanson.

ISBN-13: 978-1492836483

ISBN-10: 1492836486

Dedicated to my dear friend Clare.
Parted by the miles but close in our hearts.

Disclaimer:

This is a work of fiction. Names, characters, businesses, places, events, and incidents are either the products of the author's imagination or used in a fictitious manner. Any resemblance to actual persons, living or dead, or actual events is purely coincidental.

ACKNOWLEDGMENTS

Dr Ian Cockburn
Dr Richard Merritt
Jim Dash MRCVS
Lucy Richmond-Fisher
And of course my dear hubby Jim

All these people have given me their expertise and time in the production of this book. Thank you so much.

CONTENTS

Acknowledgments	6
Chapter 1	8
Chapter 2	26
Chapter 3	43
Chapter 4	56
Chapter 5	71
Chapter 6	84
Chapter 7	95
Chapter 8	115
Chapter 9	127
Chapter 10	140
Chapter 11	151
Chapter 12	166
Chapter 13	177
Chapter 14	189

CHAPTER ONE
(1991)

"This is the way!"

Ralph turned in the direction of the voice. It had been a long time since anybody had been in the crypt. It was dark and dirty and Ralph had felt, rightly or wrongly, that it was about time he investigated. He had not been looking forward to going down there - old tombs were not his favourite pastime - but ever since Richard had been to visit him he had known he would have to do it. Ralph turned the beam of his torch in Simon's direction and immediately started to laugh. Simon was covered in dirt and had cobwebs in his hair.

"Simon, you look dreadful. You'll need a shower and change of clothes when we get out of here."

"Don't tell me. Laura wanted me to visit her mother on the way home. I don't think I'll be able to now. Edith will die of horror if she sees me like this."

Both men laughed and Ralph sighed.

"That policeman is a bit of a pain." he said. "I've been here for five years and nobody had even mentioned an Edward Gough to me. If he did die here it must have been a long time ago."

"If you could find out why he's asking it would help, I suppose, but do you really think he's down here?"

"Well, he's not in the graveyard, so this is our only hope. I wonder how long it is since this place had a visitor? I looked in at the door five years ago and I had assumed that one of the Vergers made regular visits down here, but I can see that I'm wrong. We'll have to get a working party together to clean up this place. I'm sure the Applebys will get something going."

"I'm sure they will, but meanwhile, shall we see if we can find the elusive Edward Gough? I want to get back into the sunlight while I'm still young enough to enjoy it!"

"OK Simon, come on then. You start over there and I'll look this side."

The two men flashed the beams of their torches around the musty crypt. Most of the tombs dated from the eighteenth century. There were none with carved figures of recumbent noblemen on the top, just plain stone slabs engraved with names and dates. The two men scrambled about in the ancient chamber reading name after name. There were in excess of 15 tombs in the large room - all of them very old. The air was stale and dusty, and occasionally one of the men would cough, sending even more dust into the atmosphere. Eventually Ralph said:

"Come on Simon, we're not going to find him in here. I can't stand this any more."

"OK, just let me read this last one. No, this is someone called Isobel Welling - died in 1794, poor old girl. She was 46. Not a bad age in those days, eh? Rhetorical, old boy - let's go!"

The two men emerged into the sunlight of the late Spring day looking like ghosts. They were grey with dust and both of them had miscellaneous cobwebs adorning their bodies and hair.

"Well, you both look suitably frightening." It was Molly, Ralph's wife, emerging from the church. "I don't know whether I'm seeing a pair of ghosts or whether you're an alternative comedy act. Come on, let's get you into the shower."

"At least it's wind and weather-tight down there" said Ralph.
"Why haven't I been in there before? Slapped wrist for the Vicar - sadly lacking in his duties. Remind me to get a cleaning party together.

There's room to hold small services down there, I'm sure they will be popular."

"Who is it you're looking for?" asked Molly.

"One Edward Gough, my dear. Richard Nightingale wants to know if he's buried here. Wouldn't tell me why – need-to-know basis," he said. "At least at the moment it is. I wonder what it's all about?"

"Well, you can ask him." said Simon, "Here he is."

Ralph and Molly turned in the direction that Simon was looking. Walking up the path of the church was a tall, broadly set man with golden red hair. Molly thought how wonderful the colour looked against the green of the churchyard. She blushed slightly at her thoughts. Here was a man who carried authority and sex appeal, and he was good looking too. She was just thinking if it were possible for a man to be ugly and still be sexy when her thoughts were broken by Richard's voice.

"Good morning, everyone. You look dreadful!" And he laughed.

"Working undercover for the police," said Ralph.

"Good morning, Inspector. I'm afraid we can't find Edward Gough for you."

"Well, I'm sure he's here somewhere," said Richard. "Have you looked everywhere?"

"Oh yes," replied Simon, "And my lungs know it this morning. We've been in the crypt. Dreadful place - full of dead people."

"Please excuse my churchwarden, Inspector," said Ralph, "His name is Simon Goodall. He's a bit lily-livered. Mind you it's not a nice place, that crypt, full of dust and cobwebs. I'm going to get it cleaned up and hold services there, so you've done me a favour by making us go down there."

"You both need a shower or something," said the policeman. "Do you mind if I wander around for a bit? It's a lovely morning and Sussex is a beautiful county at this time of year. I'd like to look at your gravestones, if I may."

"Of course, Inspector. Help yourself. And when these two have showered, come to the vicarage. I'll make you some tea." Molly wanted to be in Richard's company for a bit longer. She was fascinated by this man. Still wondering if it were possible to be ugly and have sex appeal, she smiled at this handsome man. Oh, she knew that she loved Ralph and that Richard was married - to a local school teacher too - but that did not stop her from desiring his company. "A Vicar's wife, too," she thought and turned to lead the way to the vicarage.

Richard watched with amusement as the two men walked up the path, leaving a cloud of dust in the air behind them. His face broke into a smile as he faced the graves laid out on the grass. This was one of the joys of working in the countryside. There was less rush and fuss, and now that the Spring had arrived he looked forward to an interesting Summer. When the Met boys had phoned him and asked him to find Edward Gough he had been very excited. The note that the London Police Force had received had said that if they found Edward Gough they would find the key to the current spate of murders in London. It had been assumed that the three murders had been drug related. Dealers or importers of cocaine, all in North London and, it was presumed, all related. But the note had been delivered to Hendon police station. Richard remembered the exact wording:

"Edward Gough died in Sussex hundreds ago. Find him and you have the key to the murders."

Whoever sent it, and why, remained a mystery. And why so cryptic? If someone had information, you would have thought they would just come forward. The Met thought it was someone who was on the inside of whatever was going on and that they had to protect themselves. "Thank God for a villain with a conscience," thought Richard.

Richard Nightingale had worked in the Met, but now at the rank of Detective Chief Inspector he had transferred to Market Langley some 11 years previously at the mutual request of his wife and his mother. Clare and he had no children - careers had come first, and anyway they were so wrapped up in each other that they had decided that their lifestyle was what suited them best. They were both in their early 40s so there was still a little time for children. He filed away in his mind that he must talk to Clare again about the subject, perhaps for the last time. A final decision was called for. Having filed the thought in his memory, he focused on the tombstones.

The graves were all old; he guessed that no-one had been buried there since the beginning of the twentieth century. The most up-to-date grave he found was an old lady called Sarah Goode who had died in 1901 at the age of 95. She had been buried with her husband Samuel. Samuel had died in 1876 and at last they were together in death.

Richard did not hurry round the graveyard. The sun was warm and the birds were becoming territorial. That meant lots of singing and the occasional squabble. The only other sound came from the few cars that passed the church gates. The policeman's mind made him look up at the sound of every one. Some he recognised and some he didn't, but the church was off the beaten track so not many cars passed.

Richard rounded the north corner of the church and was immediately plunged into shadow. The air was chill and the sounds of the birds were absent. Richard shivered and pulled up the collar of his jacket. There were no graves here, just a few trees that were withered from the constant cold and dark. He was about to turn back when a dome of dark green caught his eye. It stood between two trees and immediately fascinated Richard's questioning mind. As he made his way toward it, it became clear that it was ivy, glossy and brooding. Richard stood beside it and was instantly excited. The ivy covered what appeared to be a headstone. It was the right shape and size but could not be seen at all under the all-engulfing plant.

Richard pulled the ivy away at a topmost corner and sure enough underneath was a stone slab. It looked very old and had crumbled, mostly due to the invasive nature of the ivy. Before he gave in to his impulses to tear the ivy away, Richard stopped. He would have to speak to Ralph and Simon. He couldn't go around vandalising graves, even if they were in a bad state of repair. Richard glanced around him. There was nothing else that was obviously a grave on this side of the church. There must be a reason for that. Even if this grave were as old as it appeared to be, grave sites must have been at a premium, even two hundred years ago. This was not a welcoming part of the churchyard, but it did seem strange that this was the only tomb.

After this curt glance at his surroundings Richard retraced his steps around to the eastern side of the church and into the sunshine. The warmth of the sun fell on his shoulders and he stood taller. He made his way across this cheerful part of the churchyard to the vicarage. The door was ajar and he peered in.

"Hello" he called, "Can I come in?"

"In here," came Ralph's reply.

Richard followed the sound of Ralph's voice to the large kitchen. The three of them were seated around the pine table. Ralph and Simon looked cleaner and both sported wet hair. Molly was busy at the percolator making coffee and a large pot of tea steamed gently on the table.

"You look a bit better" said Richard.

"Feel better too." replied Ralph, "Sit down Inspector. Cup of tea or would you like to wait for the coffee?"

"I'll wait for the coffee please. It smells delicious. What is it?"

"Cinnamon," replied Molly. "I buy it at the Mill House. They have a lot of different flavours."

"Clare goes there for cheesecake." Richard loved the confections that the two ladies at the Mill House made. "I'll have to ask her to buy some coffee. I'd like to try some others too."

Simon laughed. "You two sound like a section of the WI."

"I'll have you know, Simon," Molly bristled, "that I'm a member of the WI and we do more than talk about coffee and cheesecake. Why, only last week...."

"OK, I'm sorry!" Simon put his hands up in surrender, and Ralph chuckled.

"Don't you start," he said, "I said something similar yesterday and got a fifteen minute speech about Sierra Leone. Take it from me, old man, the WI is alive and well and working in West Downfold."

"I'm very glad to hear it." laughed Richard, "What would England be coming to without the gentle strength of its ladies?"

Molly placed the coffee pot on the table. The aroma was out of this world.

"Yes, please!" Simon and Richard spoke together.

"Well, I expect you'd like some cinnamon toast too!" laughed Molly.

"Now that you come to mention it..." Ralph knew that cinnamon toast was not an impossibility for his talented wife.

"OK, it'll be five minutes." Molly went to one of the cupboards and started busying herself about the cooker.

Richard was full of admiration. "Your wife is a genius" he said to Ralph. "You are just amazing, Molly," he said.

Molly felt her face flush. Now she felt guilty about the way she had been thinking earlier. She felt such a surge of pride - wrong for a Christian - that this very attractive man had paid her a complement. The toast was ready in no time, and as she served it to the three men at her table, she felt immense satisfaction that she could so easily do the things that some women struggled to do. Molly had always been a homemaker, and now that the twins were at University she found that she had the time to pamper Ralph and to keep the many and various visitors to the vicarage fed and entertained.

Ralph beamed at his wife between mouthfuls.

"You are wonderful, Molly," he said.

"Now then," she replied, "Or my head will be too big to go through the door." She laughed. Although it was nice to receive complements, especially from Ralph, she had to remember that she loved to keep people happy and feeding them was one of the ways she could do it.

"Ralph," Richard sounded a little more business-like, "Whose is the grave on the north side of the church that's covered in ivy?"

"Ah." Ralph put his elbows on the table and leaned forward, "Nobody is entirely sure," he continued. "We have cleared the ivy from time to time and the stone is so old that most of the lettering has worn off. Whoever it is, it must be very old. You don't find stone with that state of wear much after 1850. I think it must be the beginning of the 19th century or so. There are rumours that a warlock was buried here at the end of the 18th century and common talk has always been that this grave is the one. Nobody wants their loved ones buried on the north side of the church. The cold and wind there is one of the reasons but the presence of that grave is a bigger deterrent."

"What was his name?" asked Richard, his imagination now fired.

"Ertol," said Ralph. "At least that was the name he used in his animal practices. There's a book about him in the library in Market Langley. I haven't read all of it, but if you are interested they might even let you borrow it. Usually, it's kept for reference only. It's so old they won't let it out of their sight, but if you pull rank, you never know, they might just let you take it home."

"I'm surprised you haven't gone into this in more detail," said Richard.

Simon, who had been very quiet, spoke up, " I know a bit about him." he offered. Everybody in the room immediately turned their attention to the churchwarden.

"Well..." said Molly.

"Ertol was only the name he used "professionally", if you like to call it that. If he were alive today he would have been called a horse whisperer. He came to West Downfold in 1788, no-one knows from where. He was on the village green one morning in his 'robes most glorious', as the book says. Apparently he was tall and angular, with a 'face of death and eyes aflame'. I take it that he had a skull-like face and piercing eyes. For all intents and purposes he terrified everybody. There's an old etching of him in the book. It makes him look like a wraith or some sort of devilish figure. But he had charm. A couple of the local girls were said to have borne his children, although what happened to the children the book doesn't say. Neither of the girls married - I suppose no-one wanted a warlock's cast-off. Churchwardens are not supposed to talk like this, I know, but the morals of the people at that time were a bit convoluted. There were many children born out of wedlock, but the fathers very rarely married the women who had them, and of course, nobody else married them either. So the attraction of this man must have been very great for not one, but two, women, at least, to have fallen for his charms and risked their future happiness just to sleep with him. Anyway, I ramble on. He died in 1801 and was buried in great haste here in the churchyard. We have to assume that the grave on the north side of the church is the one because there are no other graves that old here. What else do you want to know?"

"Well, Simon, you are a fountain of knowledge," Ralph was impressed.

"What sort of things did he do?" asked Richard. "Did he prepare medicines for horses and did he treat other kinds of animal?"

"An unhealthy interest being shown here," commented Ralph, "I'm not sure that we want to let this into the conversation."

"Don't be silly dear" said Molly, "Ralph is a bit loath to let the Devil into his conversations, Richard, but I always say that the Devil can't work unless you let him in. Talking about him won't do any harm. We all know he's there, so what's the problem?"

Simon shrugged his shoulders. "With Ralph's permission," he continued, "Ertol wasn't a warlock at all, really - that's just the reputation he got. After all, apparently his potions worked on the animals. All sorts of animal too. At least, there is documented evidence that he cured all sorts of animals. He was a sort of early vet. Although he appeared very frightening, he was said to be "kind to the young and very aged". Although they do say his temper was dreadful and he did curse people who made him angry."

"So, a slightly benign vet, then" said Richard.

"So it seems, but people were afraid of him" continued Simon. "Why don't you have a look at the book? There's a whole load of stuff in it that I can't remember."

"I think I will." Richard was very interested now. However tenuous the link, he felt that Ertol might be able to lead him to Edward Gough. He hadn't thought that Gough lived that long ago, but there was nothing to lead him to believe that this could not be the case. A modern murder story might have 18th century links. And the note in London did say that Gough died "hundreds ago".

The conversation reverted to church business for the month and the cleaning of the crypt. Richard could not wait to get to the library in Market Langley, but he liked these people. They were gentle and funny. A far cry from the people he ran into most of the time during his duties at the police station. When finally the pile of cinnamon toast had been consumed, Molly offered more tea and coffee and Richard took his leave of them reluctantly.

"Must chase down some criminals," he said with some sadness at having to leave.

"Well, goodbye Richard," said Ralph offering his hand to the policeman. "We'll be seeing you soon, we hope"

"Indeed you will. Don't see me out, I'll wander through the graveyard and go the back way to the car. Goodbye Simon, thanks for the story so far. Bye-bye Molly, thanks for the marvellous repast. I'll come again if I may."

"Of course Inspector. Goodbye for now."

Molly really wanted to give Richard a kiss on the cheek but she resisted the temptation and the policeman left the vicarage. The three left in the kitchen watched him through the open window as he walked across the green grass, his golden hair alight in the sun.

"What a lovely man." Molly finally said it.

"I can see you're going to have to watch her, old friend," said Simon laughing.

Ralph chuckled. "I know. Not every day you meet such a nice police officer." said Ralph. "Come on Molly, I'll do the washing up. You and Simon can get about your other duties if you like. Simon, ring the Applebys if you would and ask them about a cleaning party for the crypt."

"Thank you, darling." Molly wanted to go into Market Langley to do some shopping, and was glad of the offer of washing up.

"I wonder whether the Inspector will find out anything about Edward Gough through this?" said Simon.

"I don't know, but he's certainly interested in our friend Ertol," replied Ralph.

"No doubt he will be back to share something with us" said Molly. "Meanwhile, I suggest we concentrate on the matters in hand and go our separate ways."

The three of them parted company: Simon and Molly in their respective cars and Ralph to the kitchen sink.

Richard was by now half way to Market Langley. He wanted to find out more about the mysterious Ertol.

Chapter Two

Richard's visit to the library was put off by a call from his car phone. It was Keane, his Sergeant.

"Are you there guv?"

"I thought I had been left in peace for too long," said Richard, "What is it, Keane?"

"Where are you? Can you come back to the station in the next half hour? The old man wants to see you."

"What does he want? I was on my way to the town anyway, I'll be there in about 15 minutes."

"Thanks guv. See you soon."

The quiet country roads were very beautiful in the warm sunshine. The catkins were almost in bloom and the young green leaves were uncurling in the warmth. Richard sighed. He turned on his tape deck and chose his tape carefully. This called for The Pastoral Suite he thought. Richard loved classical music. He was not a snob about it. He played the popular classics as well as the more obscure pieces that classical buffs seemed to prefer. He did not pontificate about his music, he just enjoyed it. His mind contained a picture of Superintendent Fisher whom Keane referred to as "the old man". The piece of music and Fisher's face did not merge too successfully. Fisher was in his middle fifties with a fleshy face. He wore his skin like an ill fitting coat. Broken veins covered his cheeks and nose. He had little hair and his eyes were such a pale blue that they looked faded. Altogether Richard found the image of the man incongruous. He pushed it from his thoughts and let the music flow over him. Ertol would have to wait for a while, at least until he had seen Fisher.

The country lanes gave way to the inevitable concrete of the town, although Market Langley was the sort of market town that Americans called "quaint". There were Tudor beams and thatched roofs along every road and the streets were narrow and winding. The police station stood back from the road and although it was not thatched and there was not a Tudor beam in sight, it still carried the air of age and stability that all very old buildings exuded. Nightingale pulled into the car park at the back of the building and reluctantly turned the music off. He sat in the driver's seat for a few seconds and looked up at his office window on the first floor of the station. The blinds were pulled down and he knew that Keane would be waiting for him to brief him on what Fisher wanted. Reluctantly he opened the door of the car and got out. If Keane was up to his usual standard he would have heard Richard's car and would have put the kettle on. "Good old Keane," thought Richard and smiled to himself. He made his way through the police station. It was surprisingly quiet. He saw very few of his colleagues on his familiar journey up the stairs to the waiting Keane.

"Morning, guv."

This was Keane's usual salutation to Richard, and this morning he did not disappoint. The kettle was bubbling to a boil and Keane made the coffee. Not up to Molly's standard and Keane did not run to cinnamon toast, but it was a good filter coffee and made the mood of the morning very mellow for both men.

"So, what does Fisher want?" asked Nightingale.

"Sorry, guv. No idea. I did try to get some information out of him, but he's staying very tight-lipped."

"Well, I suppose I'd better scurry along to his office. If I'm not back in an hour send a search party!"

Both men laughed and Richard drained his coffee cup.

"Don't get eaten!" was Keane's parting shot as Richard closed the door of the office.

Fisher was always long-winded, and used 20 words when five would do. Richard would really need to be rescued if he wasn't back in his office in an hour, but Keane knew what he had to do if Richard was away from his desk for too long.

Richard knocked on the door of Fisher's office.

"Come in." the reply was terse and Richard knew immediately that he was in for a rough ride.

Inside the office it was warm. The sun shone through the large windows and reflected off the oak panelling. Richard felt that Fisher used the wall panelling and the large oak desk as a status symbol. It boosted Fisher's ego and it seemed to Richard that Fisher hid behind the impression that the office exuded.

"Good morning, Nightingale. Sit down."

Richard sat in one of the leather chairs opposite Fisher and waited.

"I won't beat about the bush, Richard."

Nightingale was all attention. Fisher rarely used his Christian name. This meant that Fisher was going to confide in him.

"There's been another death in Hendon. During the night. The local force were notified at 6.30 this morning. The victim's brother found the body when he called round to get him up for work. Male, IC1, 32 years old. Nothing to indicate foul play on the body, just like the others. Normally we would put it down to natural causes, but there was a note left with the body just like the others. No fingerprints anywhere. No disturbance in the room and nobody heard anything."

"What did the note say?"

"We haven't got the transcript yet, but Lambert at Hendon gave me the gist. Like the others this was very odd. It said that chummy had been killed as an act of revenge - something about old scores to settle. I should have more information about the whole thing by this afternoon. There'll be a post mortem of course, but you can be sure that there will be no sign of a suspicious death. Probably be brain haemorrhage like the others. The fact is, Richard, that the Met are really stumped about these deaths. This one makes number four. The only thing they've got to go on is the anonymous note about Edward Gough. Have you got any further?"

"Not much, Reg. It seems to me that we can narrow the search down to the immediate area. That is assuming that Edward Gough was buried in a churchyard. There are no churches old enough outside this area. I know that other parts of the county are looking into this too, and it's got to be just chance if anybody comes up with something positive. We're talking about hundreds of years ago. And we don't know how many hundred. It's all very nebulous you know. I really don't know how much longer we can go on spending the time chasing this when it's almost impossible to find anything without more information."

"Doesn't it seem odd to you, Richard, that three people, possibly four, all died of brain haemorrhage, on one patch. All in their own homes with no sign of break-in or struggle. They would not even have been noticed as anything other than natural causes if it were not for the notes found with the bodies. It is obvious that the perpetrator wants us to know he killed them. But why? He could easily have got away with it unnoticed, but no, he leaves a note with each body."

Richard joined in the speculation. "And how did he, or indeed she, manage to induce a brain haemorrhage in each of them, leaving no outward signs? I think I'll pay a visit to a tame surgeon I know and get a further medical opinion. What was it that Sullivan said in his reports?"

"He has speculated that it could be a sonic disturbance to the brain. But that's spy stuff. The Ipcress File and all that."

"I didn't know that you were a fan of Michael Caine." said Richard with a smile. He knew that Fisher was not famous for his sense of humour, but he could not resist this comment.

"It's an old film, Richard," replied Fisher. "I saw it at the pictures when it first came out. I was an aspiring young copper and thought it was the most exciting thing I had ever seen. Those were the days when spying was not public domain."

"Well, I don't know whether Harry Palmer would be able to help us with this. I'll continue to search for Edward Gough, but I really don't hold out much hope."

"Not good enough, Richard". Fisher was getting aggressive now. "We really need to throw some light on this."

"But we don't know for sure whether he died here. Can we really justify spending the time looking for somebody when we are not sure he died here, or indeed, whether he existed at all? After all, the note may be a false trail."

"There is always that possibility, but this is an intriguing case. Don't you find it fascinating, Richard? I really want to come up with the answer."

"How long are we going to continue? Is there a sell-by date?"

"Another week and then I think we will have to call a halt. I hope you find Gough and that he's not somewhere else in Sussex. This case really fires me up, Richard. I really want us to find this man."

"Well, I'll give it my best shot, Reg."

Richard rose from the chair and moved towards the door.

"Keep me posted. I want results, sooner rather than later, Richard."

"OK. I'll write my report this afternoon. It'll be on your desk by tomorrow morning."

"Good. Thanks, Richard."

Nightingale closed Fisher's office door behind him. The old man was really caught up in this case. Perhaps there was a bit of dark romance in him after all. Harry Palmer indeed! Richard now wanted to find Gough even more than he did before. If he didn't find him it would be a biggest waste of police time that he had come across for years. On the evidence of a note that might be a red herring, half the constabulary in Sussex, East and West, were looking for a man who might not have existed. Richard knew there was something that Fisher was not telling him. Fisher was not the kind of copper who let the romance of the Ipcress File carry him away. There was something deeper going on. Richard wanted to know what it was. He would get a summons after Fisher had read his report, and he was determined to probe further. Today had been the wrong time, but tomorrow he would find out.

Richard's thoughts had carried him along the corridor to his own office. Keane was on the phone when Richard entered the room.

"Yes, sir, I'll pass the message on. Thank you for letting us know. Good bye"

Keane hung up.

"Well? What did he want?"

"Me first. Who was that."

"Oh, it was Ralph Beddows. He wondered if you would like to go to lunch tomorrow. Wants you to call him back."

"That's decent of him. I'll call him this afternoon. If his wife's cooking is up to the standard of her cinnamon toast, then I'm in for a treat."

"Now me, what *did* the old man want?"

"Just a chivvy along for the Gough thing. Can't understand it Keane. It seems on the face of it to be a total waste of time. Can you really see us finding a man who died some hundreds of years ago. And even if we do, what will that tell us? I know the deaths are a mystery and we may be dealing with some kind of real nutter, but I really don't know why the old man's making such a big thing of finding Gough. After all, it may be a total wrong-footer."

"Ours is not to reason why, guv."

"Oh, but it is, Keane." Richard was surprised that his sergeant had learned so little from him.

"We don't follow orders blindly, Keane, you know that. We question and lead our own ground, moral and legal. I thought I'd taught you better than that."

"Sorry, guv. It's just that nobody seems to be doing the standard police work on these murders. We don't even know if the victims were linked. What about forensics at the scene and on the victim? We need to know more. I've just given up thinking about it. The whole case seems a bit iffy."

"Don't think I hadn't thought of all that, Keane. I put in a call to Lambert at Hendon. I'm waiting for him to get back to me. The questions I want to ask are the same ones that Fisher skirted round earlier in the case. I'll get to the bottom of this. We need to know, Keane."

"Are you here for the rest of the day, guv? I wanted to go and have a look at the Registers of Births, Marriages and Deaths at the Civic Offices."

"Good idea. I'm heading for the library round the corner. Nothing to do with the case, but there's some history I want to look up."

"Did someone famous once live here, then?"

"No, I don't think you could call him famous. I only found out about him today. It's a man who is believed to be buried in St's Peter and Paul's churchyard. I've got a report to write for the old man this afternoon and a sandwich and a good book will settle the brain nicely. I'm sure someone must have searched Somerset House early in the case, Keane, but ten out of ten for effort."

"Well, if we're talking about hundreds of years ago, I'm not sure it would be in Somerset House, and it's likely that the Met know this, so I'm going to have a look."

"OK, while you're gone I'll make a few phone calls. People to talk to, you know, and a report to write. I'll drop into the library before I go home."

"Right, I'm off. Back in a couple of hours, I hope."

Nightingale's hopes of going to the library had been dashed again. He really ought to find out a few things. Keane was right. Good old fashioned police hard graft was what was needed. As Keane disappeared out of the door, Nightingale picked up the phone. He dialled Ralph Beddows' number. Molly answered,

"St Peter and Paul's vicarage."

"Hello Molly, Richard Nightingale."

"Well hello Richard. I'm afraid Ralph is out at the moment, but I can give him a message."

"I don't necessarily have to talk to Ralph," replied Richard. "He very kindly asked me to lunch tomorrow and the hors d'oeuvres of cinnamon toast was just too much. I'd be delighted to come."

"That's great," Molly had to stop herself sounding excited. "Is there anything you don't eat?"

"Not much, but I have an allergy to sea food. Everything, I'm afraid. Can you handle that."

"How awful for you. But it doesn't present too much of a problem. I'll keep the menu a surprise, shall I? Can you be here at one and we'll eat at about one thirty?"

"Wonderful," replied Richard. He was looking forward to tasting Molly's cooking again. "See you at one tomorrow."

"Bye bye, see you tomorrow."

Richard hung up the phone and smiled to himself. This was just what he needed to get his mind off this case. The diversion into the history of Ertol was something he could uncover in his spare time. What a magical story to have surrounding the church! He would find out about the horse whisperer. Perhaps he could ask Ralph a bit more tomorrow. And he must get to the library eventually.

Richard's next phone call was to Lambert. Mr Neville Lambert was a surgeon of some note at Guy's Hospital in London. He worked for the police in all sorts of medical capacities from being called as an expert witness to a friendly opinion over the phone when one was needed.

Richard got through to him fairly easily. He happened to be at Hendon police station. Lambert sounded tired over the phone.

"Hello Richard. No wicked for the peaceful is there."

"Hello Neville. Can I pick your brains about the murders on your patch?"

"Fire away old man. I'll tell you all I can."

"Did you see the bodies?"

"Yes, well two of them. I went out of my way to sit in on the post mortems. I missed the first one. Wrong place at the wrong time, but was determined not to miss the rest. I'm sitting in on the PM of what is probably the fourth this afternoon. What can I tell you?"

"It was definitely brain haemorrhage, wasn't it? I mean, there's no doubt, is there?"

"None at all Richard. No outward or internal signs of a fight or struggle. Sudden, instant death. I'm as foxed as you are."

"Please forgive me, Neville, but there are no puncture wounds anywhere that could indicate injected drugs to induce a brain haemorrhage?"

"No Richard. No puncture wounds were found."

"And what was the time of death? Did it vary between cases, or were they all killed in the night, or even at two o'clock in the afternoon?"

"It varies Richard. One was estimated at 7.00am, one at midnight and the other was 8.00pm. There just doesn't seem to be a link between them. Oh, apart from one thing and I don't know whether you consider it significant."

"Yes."

"They all suffered from skin conditions. One had psoriasis and two suffered from eczema. All in various stages of manifestation. One with really bad eczema, he was also an asthmatic. The other two in some form of remission but with old lesion scars."

"Well, how does that tie up with a brain haemorrhage? It's worth filling in the grey matter but I suppose it may be a coincidence. Thanks Neville, if you think of anything else that may be useful, please call me. And I look forward to hearing from you after the PM this afternoon."

'I'll give you a ring, bye Richard."

Nightingale sat and pondered. His report would not write itself. He gathered the wherewithal he would need to write it and tucked his head down to the task.

Keane, meanwhile, was at the Registrar's office. The very comely young lady who took him to the archives section brought a bright note into his task. All the oldest documents were on microfilm. Keane supposed this was to protect what must be very fragile pieces of paper. It seemed an age before suddenly and completely unexpectedly he found a death certificate and there was the name Edward St. John Gough. He had died in 1801. A light came on in his mind. Keane purchased a copy of the death certificate and decided that there was no time like the present. The name of the informant who registered the death was also called Edward Gough. A son perhaps? He decided to take his trophy back to the police station and have a conference with Nightingale before he did any more, but he was so pleased with what he had found that he almost kissed the young woman who was helping him. The paper tucked safely in his inside pocket Keane beat a hasty retreat to the Station.

He arrived just as Nightingale was crossing the last T of his report. He burst through the door of their office and Nightingale jumped visibly.

"You ought to be kind to old men," he said with his hand on his chest, "I know you are on your way to being promoted to Inspector, but please don't get rid of me yet! I'll just put this report on Fisher's desk and you can tell me why you look of damn pleased with yourself."

There was no-one in Fisher's office to Richard's relief. He placed his missive front and centre of the desk and beat a hasty retreat.

Keane's discovery filled him with hope. Now, was the Edward Gough they were seeking the father or the son? Best to be absent when Fisher returned, so Richard decided to make himself scarce. Off he set for the library leaving Keane to catch up on their paperwork. He smiled. At last they might be getting somewhere.

Chapter Three

The library was a large and imposing building. It had been the home of the Ford family for 100 years. When the final member of the family died in 1974 he had bequeathed it to the Council. He had no relatives to care for it and he guessed that no one person or family could manage the upkeep, so in his will he had given it to the local authority with the proviso that it be used for the public.

It had a grey stone façade with a grand front door, today left open to welcome all who came there. Inside, the spacious hallway boasted flowers and a large mahogany desk. Penny Wilson was sitting behind the desk.

"Hello, Penny. I wonder if you could help me with an old book?"

"I hope so, Mr Nightingale. What are you looking for?"

"A history of the local area. Including some information about a man that lived here - name of Ertol."

"I haven't heard anyone refer to him for such a long time. What a character he was, by all accounts! Yes, we do have a local history, would you like to come with me?"

Nightingale followed Penny up the grand sweeping staircase that dominated the hallway, and he wondered what it must have been like to live there and how they had kept it clean. There was an army of council cleaners who looked after it now, but the Fords must have had a large staff. Penny took Nightingale along a corridor and producing a large key, unlocked a door. Once inside, the years seemed to melt away. They were surrounded with shelves from floor to ceiling, each shelf crammed with old tomes. The smell of the room was of cold clean air. Nightingale knew immediately that this was some sort of air conditioning designed to stop the documents that were so lovingly stored from crumbling to dust. There was a table and two chairs at the far end of the room. Penny made her way to the table. She opened a small drawer and took out two pairs of white cotton gloves.

"You'll have to wear these when you touch any book in here," explained Penny. "They stop the grease and anything else you have on your hands from getting onto the pages."

They both donned the gloves and Penny went straight to a shelf three quarters of the way along the row and to the middle shelf. She placed the book she had retrieved on the table and carefully started turning the pages. The book was not printed but hand written.

Nightingale marvelled at the precise and beautiful writing and could have just looked at it all day.

"Here we are," said Penny. "You should find what you want on these two pages. Please, if you need to turn a page, do it most carefully. I'll be back in half an hour to see how you're getting on."

"Thanks, Penny," said Nightingale "Cross my heart I will be very careful. This book is so beautiful I would hate to damage it."

Penny left Nightingale alone with the precious tome. He ran his gloved hand gently across the page.

"How many people had it taken to make this historic book?" he thought. "And the loving care it must have taken to write it, so meticulously and beautifully."

He started to read, and the story the book held was fascinating. Sure enough, Simon had been right. Ertol appeared on the village green in West Downfold one morning with a brightly painted horse-drawn caravan. Over the following days and weeks he slowly began to make it apparent that he could cure animals of illnesses. It started when one of the local children brought him an injured owl she had found in the wood. Ertol took it in, and within a week it was fit and he took it back to where it had been found. The child was delighted, and word soon spread of the event. One of the local land owners, Lord Deare, heard the story and sent word for Ertol to visit him to look at a horse. Ertol mixed a potion for the horse after examining it and visited every day to talk to the horse. Within 10 days the horse was back to pulling a plough, and the land owner was so pleased he invited Ertol to use one of his fields for his caravan. So Ertol had left the green and lived with the Lord. Almost immediately he was acceptable to the locals and all manner of animals were brought to him.

There seemed to be a gap in information after that because the book then spoke of a son being born to a local woman called Constance. She and Ertol were not married, and her family had thrown her out. Apparently she gave the child to Ertol and then threw herself into the local river and drowned. It seemed to Nightingale that things had come on since then. Nobody today would react badly to an unmarried mother in the same way that the girl's family had back then. Well, not many, anyway.

The child had lived with Ertol for 12 years, when a candle had been knocked over and the caravan destroyed by fire. The child, who was called Edward Gough, was killed in the fire. Some of the locals though that Constance's family had been responsible for the fire. Constance had a sister called Patience who was married to Jez Waters, a local cowman. They had two children. There was no more information other than that Ertol lived in a barn on Lord Deare's land for the rest of his life. It seems he lived there happily in an unwed state with a woman called Louisa. Nightingale thought it was safe to assume that there were other children, but none of them was mentioned by name. There were more notes about animals who were cured, and it seemed from the narrative that nothing quite so spectacular happened again in Ertol's lifetime, but at least Nightingale had found Edward Gough. He was Ertol's son. He made a lot of handwritten notes about his reading and when Penny came back into the room was sitting smiling secretively to himself.

"Did it help you, Inspector?" she asked

"More than I could have hoped. Do you know that you might have been instrumental in solving a series of murders?"

"Well I never," said Penny "I don't suppose you will tell me how?"

"Sorry Penny, I can't. But I think this book might be used again in this investigation. I'll let you know if I need it again. As you can see

I've left it undamaged and I think that deserves a gold star!" laughed Nightingale

"Tick, v.g. I think. I'll put it away and wait for you to come back" said the amused Penny. "Can you leave your gloves on the table, they will have to be laundered now."

"You do guard your precious books carefully, don't you?"

Nightingale was impressed by the meticulous way Penny looked after the books.

"Oh, yes." She was surprised, "I had to go on a course about the care of the books in here. They are the town's heritage. They will still be here when you and I are long dead."

"I hope they will," replied Nightingale. "Thank you, Penny, I'll see you soon."

Nightingale was delighted with what he had found. However, it made the case even more complicated. How could he link a 12-year-old boy with the current murders? He would have a brain-storming session with Keane when he got back to the station. He would be sorry when Keane was elevated to Inspector, as he surely would be one day - they bounced off each other so well.

When Nightingale got back to the police station Keane was already there. He was very excited.

"You look like a dog with two tails," laughed Nightingale,

"Well, I feel like one. I've found Edward Gough!" Keane said this with a flourish in his voice.

"Well, so have I," said a surprised Nightingale. This was amazing, the two men both finding someone they had been looking for for weeks, and at more or less the same time.

Keane broke into a broad grin. "You tell me what you've found and then we can compare."

Nightingale told his story about Ertol and his son called Edward Gough, Constance and the fire. Keane found the whole story enthralling.

"Someone should make a film about this," he said.

"You're right, it's pure Hollywood, isn't it?" Nightingale began to wonder who on earth would play the part of Ertol. It would have to be someone with great charisma and painfully thin! His thoughts were interrupted when Keane showed him the death certificate he had found.

"So, it looks as it both of them were called Edward Gough. What a nuisance. But I can only suppose that the murderer is someone related to both of them. A family member, perhaps?"

Nightingale pondered. After so much time not being able to find Edward Gough, now they had two of them.

"What do you think, Keane?" asked Nightingale.

"Well, it must be someone who knows about both of them. Perhaps a distant relative. But why they are doing it is Chinese to me. After all this time, when the two of them had been forgotten by most people, why is this happening?"

Nightingale would not have known about Ertol if Simon hadn't had a mind that stored information. Nightingale wondered who would be left who knew about him in 50 years time. Perhaps this case would become well known and they would stay in people's minds forever, like Guy Fawkes, remembered for something that went back an awfully long time.

Nightingale's phone rang. It was Fisher requesting his company.

"See you later, Keane. Hope it's not more reminiscences about Michael Caine!"

Nightingale tapped on Fisher's door.

"Come in, Richard. Take a seat. I found your report very interesting, but of course, we lack anything concrete."

"Not any more, sir. Both Keane and I have found evidence that two people, we believe a father and son, called Edward Gough lived here in the late 1700s. I will write an addendum to my report and bring you up to date. We have a lot of interesting historical events that may bear significance to this case."

"So, it was worth it in the end. Yes, please do let me have a look at it in writing. And let me have yours and Keane's evidence. I won't make you tell me now, it's high time we all went home. But write it up in the morning and leave it for me. I'm at a conference tomorrow. Modern Policing, for my sins. At least we get a decent lunch at these events."

"OK, sir, it'll be on your desk when you get back, but I tell you, it's a fascinating story. See you tomorrow, have a good evening and a good conference tomorrow."

Fisher pulled a face. Nightingale laughed, he had never seen Fisher so animated.

"Night, Richard. Think yourself lucky that you don't have to attend too many conferences."

"Oh, I do, sir, I do." And with a smile Nightingale made his way back to his office. Keane was busy making notes of what they had found out.

"Don't want to forget anything, sir."

"Good idea, Keane. The old man wants me to write it up tomorrow, so making notes is a very good idea. When you've done that, go home, I'm sure June will be pleased to see you."

"What a good idea. Neither of us has been home early for a long time. You going now?"

"I thought I would. I'm even in time to take Clare to the pictures, she always knows what's on. I'll ask if there's anything she wants to see."

"Well, good night, sir. See you in the morning."

Nightingale left the station feeling pleased with himself. Now all they had to do was to find out which Edward Gough the notes referred to. After lunch at the vicarage tomorrow, he'd pay a visit to Simon to find out if he knew any more. He certainly seemed to be knowledgeable about Ertol. Wait until he told Simon that he knew Ertol's real name!

When he reached home, one of their cats, Bramble, ran to greet him.

"Hello, Bramble, old boy. Is your mummy home yet? Probably not or you wouldn't be around me asking for food. You see, I do know your tricks. Come on let's go inside."

Sure enough, Clare was not home yet. Nightingale put the kettle on to boil and busied himself feeding the three cats. They were all different ages and had all been rescued from cat sanctuaries over the years. They were Richard and Clare's surrogate children. They both knew that and did not mind at all. They would not have children now, and had stopped talking about it. They enjoyed the life they had and did not need a child to make it complete. While Nightingale was pouring the boiling water into the pot, he heard Clare's key in the lock.

"In here, darling!" Nightingale called.

Clare walked into the kitchen carrying an arm full of exercise books.

"Hello, Richard. Had a good day? Have you fed the cats? Is that tea I see?"

"Yes, yes and yes." Replied Nightingale and smiled at his wife. He still found her beautiful, and when they had been apart all day, the first time he saw her he marvelled at his good fortune.

"Does that pile of books mean you are busy tonight? I thought we could go to the cinema."

"What a lovely idea, but I'm afraid I've got to mark these tonight. Shame, they've got a rerun of The Graduate at The Pavilion. I enjoyed it the first time around, but I would like to have seen it again."

"Tell you what. You mark your books, I'll cook and then we can get up to naughtiness, how does that sound."

"Great," said Clare, and she kissed him on the cheek. "But you'd better have a shave first, you're very scratchy."

Nightingale poured the tea, humming quietly to himself. Chutney, their ginger tom sat on a chair next to Nightingale and closed his eyes. All was right with the world, and worries seemed a long way away. Nightingale rubbed Chutney's head absently, this had got to be better than working for the Met at his age. He had loved it while he was younger, but the move to Sussex was a very good idea as he grew less quick to react. Of course Keane did not notice and Nightingale himself hardly noticed, but when life and limb were at stake it mattered to the perpetrator. Yes, if he could unwind the Ertol business before there was another murder, he would be very pleased, and still humming to himself, he carried the tea into the sitting room.

CHAPTER FOUR

Nightingale and Keane arrived at the police station at the same time the following morning. Nightingale was still humming and Keane shot him a sideways look.

"I've never known you to be musical. I know you like your classical music in the car, but unless I'm mistaken, that's Bali Hai from South Pacific!"

"I'm surprised you know it, Keane. The film was issued in the 50s."

Keane laughed. "My Mum told me about it," he chuckled.

"Well, my life is great, we are on to Edward Gough and I just feel happy."

'You've got a report to write for The Old Man, don't forget."

"Yes, and I have a lunch engagement at the vicarage of Saints Peter and Paul too, so I think I am going to have a good day"

Nightingale wrote his report covering everything pertinent and took it along to Fisher's office. Surprisingly he was there.

"Come in." answered Fisher to Nightingale's knock on the door. "Ah, Richard, come in and sit down."

Nightingale handed him the report, which he read immediately, while Nightingale was in the room.

"Well, this is interesting stuff. All we need now is to catch chummy before he strikes again, but of course, we don't know why he – or she – is doing this, and whether there is any order to the victims."

"Absolutely. I'm going to try to find out whether Ertol had any more children by his muse, Louisa. I expect he did, but I'll take myself along to the library tomorrow to see if they have any more about Edward Gough, either father or son."

"You know, sometimes I think it would be good if I were a DCI again. Getting my hands in the dough with the hope that the bread will rise. Sometimes I envy you, Richard. All I seem to do is sit behind my desk being responsible for things that often get out of control."

"How do you mean, sir? I thought we ran a tight ship here."

"We do, by and large. But you take this Ertol business. I was about to pull the plug and you come up with all the information we need to justify keeping the case open. And now we know that it originated on our patch, it shouldn't be too difficult to find out more."

"Well, it's so long ago that there might not be too much information. I'm going out to the church shortly, I'll see if I can get a look at the parish records."

"Good man. I'm on my way to the conference now. But find me when you can and bring me up to date."

Nightingale wandered slowly back to his office, Keane was on the phone.

"Here he is now, I'll pass you over." Then to Nightingale, "It's Ralph Webster."

"Hello, Ralph. Is something wrong?"

"I'm not sure, Richard. It's Simon, my churchwarden. He was supposed to come to the church this morning, but didn't. I went to his house and can get no reply. All the curtains are drawn. Will you come over?"

"Straight away Ralph. I'll bring my Sergeant too."

Nightingale hung up the phone.

"Come on Keane, we might have a suspicious death at worse, or someone taken seriously ill. We'll go in my car."

The two of them drove to the vicarage of the church to be met by Ralph and Molly standing in the front garden.

"I'll bring my car," said Ralph. "You stay here, Molly. I'll let you know the news as soon as we know anything."

The two cars drove to Simon's house. Sure enough the curtains were all drawn. It was a lovely flint cottage on the far side of West Downfold. There were even roses growing around the front door. If the situation had been different, Nightingale would have liked to have a look around. He didn't know at that moment, but he was going to get a look round anyway. Nightingale knocked on the door. There was no answer.

"You go round the back, Keane."

"OK, guv. I hope this is not what I think it is."

"Yes, Keane." Then to Ralph, "Don't ever let anybody know what I am about to do. Strictly unethical."

Ralph frowned in bewilderment and then gave a small smile as Nightingale took an enormous bunch of keys out of his pocket.

"I must have something here that will get us in."

Nightingale looked at the lock, it was a standard Chubb. On the selection of the second key he tried, the lock gave a small click and the door swung open. He met Keane in the hall.

"Back door unlocked, guv. I don't think he went to bed last night or he would have locked it."

Nightingale pushed open the door on his right. It turned out to be the sitting room. They didn't have to go very far into the room to find Simon slumped on the sofa. Keane felt for a pulse.

"Nothing, sir."

Ralph was right behind them. He came forward and took Simon's hand.

"I think he's dead, sir," said Keane.

"But what could have killed him? He was so fit! He used to run every morning and swim three times a week."

Keane slipped quietly to Nightingale's side and handed him a piece of paper. Nightingale took it, read it, and put it in his pocket.

Keane went to the phone and rang for an ambulance. Nightingale turned to Ralph.

"We've got to secure the scene, Ralph. Why don't you go back to the vicarage, and we'll follow you in a while?"

'What... Oh yes, I suppose so. What am I going to tell Molly and the PCC? Oh, this is dreadful. Where is his wife? I don't know how this could have happened."

Ralph left the cottage still mumbling under his breath. Keane rang for Forensics and a uniformed man to stand guard.

Nightingale took the paper out of his pocket and turned to Keane.

"Where was this, Keane?"

"Under his left hand, sir. Same words almost as the others."

Nightingale read it out loud: "Another one for Edward."

"Well, the case has come to us, now. We can really get our teeth into it."

The ambulance arrived and the forensic team straight afterwards. The photographer busied himself taking pictures, and the forensic team got to work. There were two wine glasses on the table and two empty wine bottles. Nothing was disturbed, so there was no struggle. The police surgeon could find no obvious cause of death. The post mortem would be tomorrow morning, so Nightingale satisfied himself he would have to wait until then.

"Come on, Keane, let's see if Molly knows where we can find Simon's wife."

The two policemen drove back to the vicarage. The front door was open and Nightingale poked his head inside and called "Hello". Ralph appeared in the hallway.

"Come in, Richard. I don't know your name, Keane, and it seems so rude not to use it."

"David, sir."

"OK, David, come with me both of you. Molly is so upset and she can't stop crying."

He took them into his study. Two walls were completely covered with bookshelves full of books. There was a typewriter on the desk and piles of paper.

"Where is Simon's wife? She can't have been home last night - or could she?" asked Ralph.

"I wouldn't think it was his wife, Ralph. I know that most murders are committed within the family, but we have evidence that links this case with others outside our patch."

Ralph stared at Nightingale.

"What case?" He leaned forward, all attention.

"I can't tell you that at the moment I'm afraid, but rest assured this is not a family argument gone wrong. Now how do we find his wife? I don't want her returning home to find a house full of policemen."

There was a small tap on the door and Molly opened it. Her eyes were red from crying and she clutched a paper handkerchief in her hand.

"Do you want a cup of coffee? Lunch will be ready shortly. Will you stay, sergeant?"

"Yes, do stay. We can rack our brains as to where Laura is."

"I can answer that," said Molly, "She's in Somerset with their son. I know that Simon had a piece of paper with their contact details on. I saw him put it inside the telephone numbers book that Laura keeps in the kitchen."

Well, what a useful visit this had been. The three men said yes, please to coffee and Nightingale turned to Keane.

"We'll pop back to the scene after the coffee and find Laura's contact details. Then, if Ralph and Molly don't mind a quick getaway after lunch, we'll go back to the station and see if we can make contact with Mrs Goodall."

"Sounds like a plan," said Keane, "Thank you for inviting me to stay to lunch, I'm more used to sandwiches and if I'm lucky, a Pot Noodle."

"It's a pleasure, David, and I think we have a Molly special – a home-made cottage pie."

"Scrummy!" said Keane, and his face broke into an enormous smile. Molly entered the study with coffee. Not just ordinary coffee but latte, and Nightingale was amused to see that she had dusted the top of Ralph's coffee with chocolate sprinkles in the shape of a heart.

"What a lucky man!" thought Nightingale. Molly was a perfect wife for Ralph. A pleasant disposition, a thoughtful hostess and a good cook. Nightingale felt sure that the Websters were very good for the parish. He wondered why there were no children in evidence. Perhaps he would find out eventually.

They drank their coffee, which was delicious and Keane stood up and went to the bookshelves.

"Have you read all these?" he asked.

"'Fraid so," chuckled Ralph. "One thing about being a vicar is that you have to be knowledgeable."

"Rather you than me," smiled Keane. "Some of them look like tough going."

"Some of them are. If in doubt refer to the maker's handbook!" Ralph waved a Bible at him. All three men smiled and Nightingale and Keane took their leave, promising to return within the hour.

Nightingale played the 1812 Overture in the car.

"This is a bit frantic!" said Keane.

"Well, it is a celebration of victory. Think Keane, we now have our own murder case that links with the four in the Met. We can crack this, Keane. We've got a long way to go, and we will need to put our thinking heads on, but I'm sure we can do it."

"Oh, I've no doubt we can, sir, and won't the old man bask in our reflected light when we do?"

They both laughed. Fisher was very good at public relations and would come into his own if he had to announce that a murder had been solved, especially one like this.

Nightingale and Keane went back inside Simon's cottage. It didn't take long to find the contact details for Laura Goodall. The house seemed to be bursting at the seams with policeman. The rooms were quite small and appeared to be full of people. The doctor was still there.

"Hello, Richard. This is a rum do."

"How? It looks as if he got drunk and died. Although we have evidence to prove otherwise."

"Well, exactly. I'll have what's left of the wine analysed, but he shows no indication of foul play. He was in good health by the look of it, so why did he die? Come to the morgue about three and you can be in on the post mortem. I've decided to reschedule it and do it today"

"OK doc. Thanks."

The two policemen left with the piece of paper showing Laura Goodall's location. Nightingale got on the radio. He spoke to Fisher who was still not at his conference, who said he would get the Somerset police to go and tell Mrs Goodall the bad news. He could let Nightingale know when she would be back home so that he could meet her.

They drove on in silence,

"No music, sir?"

"What?" Nightingale shook himself. He had been miles away with Laura Goodall. He tried to think how he would feel if Fisher appeared at his door one day to tell him that Clare had been killed. It did not bear thinking about, he would be absolutely desolate.

"Oh, do you want some?"

"Not really. You seemed miles away sir."

"I was, Keane. Let's hope a nice lunch at the vicarage can put the steam back in the locomotive, shall we?"

"I should say!" said Keane, rubbing his hands together. "What was it? Cottage pie? What's the difference between cottage pie and shepherd's pie? Do you know?"

"As a matter of fact, I do, so there. Shepherd's pie is made with lamb and cottage pie is made with beef. It's obvious when you know the answer."

"Well, I never did." Replied Keane "So we're getting beef?"

"It seems so Keane. Are you hungry? I'm famished."

They arrived at the vicarage to see Ralph just making his way there from the church.

"Hello, Richard. Hello, David. Are you ready to eat?"

"I should say so," replied Keane.

"Lead on, Macduff!" said Nightingale with a smile.

They all trooped into the vicarage kitchen like three hungry schoolboys. The smell was wonderful. Molly was weeping quietly over the stove. Ralph rushed to her side.

"Oh, darling. Are you up to this? We can do it another day, if you prefer."

"No, it's OK. I'll be all right in a minute. Pour everybody a beer would you and I'll serve up"

"Not for us", said Nightingale. "We're working, remember."

"Would you like some pomegranate juice? There's some in the fridge."

'Oh, yes, please," replied Keane and Nightingale smiled.

"That would be smashing. Thank you," he said.

Ralph poured the drinks and Molly put the most delicious-looking pie on the table. She turned back to the stove to collect four plates that were warming there.

"Will you find Laura?" she said

"Oh, yes. We will now. I've arranged for the police local to her location to go to the house and tell her. I expect you will see her tomorrow. What an awful thing to be told."

"Absolutely." Said Molly. "I'll do all I can to help her, but it won't be easy."

"I don't expect it will. They have a son, don't they? How old is he?"

"He's 14," replied Molly. "Just the age when he needs his Dad. Oh, poor Matthew."

Ralph put his arm around her shoulders.

"It's going to be tough, but we can see them through it. We have to be strong."

Molly nodded and straightened up.

"Well boys, who'd like the first portion?"

All three men held out their plates and at last all four of them laughed.

CHAPTER FIVE

When Nightingale and Keane arrived back at the police station, Fisher was waiting in Nightingale's office. He very rarely left the womb-like confines of his wood panelling and both the CID men were surprised to see him.

"Hello, sir. Not at your conference? Are you visiting us or are you just after the chocolate biscuits?"

"Don't be facetious, Richard, this is serious."

"Sorry, sir. How can we help you?"

"There are forensic bods all over the house where our latest murder took place. How do you know it was a murder, and how is it linked to the Hendon Four?"

Keane smiled to himself. "The Hendon Four" - he would use that. A bit precious, but he liked it.

Nightingale took a plastic evidence bag from his pocket and gave it to Fisher.

"This note was under Goodall's left hand, and it links directly to the notes found in the other four murders. We've got a post mortem to attend in 20 minutes. What can I tell you in that time? You know we have found references to Edward Gough – we have more research to do with that one. We think there are two of them, a father and son. Give us a couple of days to sort it out and we might have more on that. The big question is, how did the victims die, and what can cause someone to die with absolutely no method obvious?"

"It's a tough one, Richard." Fisher looked at his watch. "You'd better high tail it over to the morgue if you're going to be there on time. I have every faith in you – that includes you too Keane. Keep me informed, and now I know you have chocolate biscuits I might come foraging while you're out."

Nightingale and Keane laughed.

"Not even time for a cup of tea," moaned Keane.

"Come on, we can have one at the morgue. Bye, sir. I'll keep you in the loop."

All three men left the office together. Fisher went to the right towards his office and Nightingale and Keane turned left to the exit and car park.

"My car," said Nightingale and the two men set off to their appointment. There was not much traffic. Nightingale sometimes wondered what would happen if the locals were suddenly subjected to the volumes of traffic regularly encountered in London and surrounds. He smiled to himself. Life was so much less stressful in Sussex. And now he had a job to get his teeth into. He started to sing Nessun Dorma – quite well, or so Keane thought. They made their way through the lanes to the morgue, which was not too far from the police station. Nightingale stopped singing as they pulled into the cart park. Keane broke into applause.

"Well done, guv. I didn't know you could sing."

"I was a member of a choir in London, but not many people have heard me sing solo. Not a word to anybody else, Keane. I don't want to be The Singing Detective. Michael Gambon did that on TV, didn't he?"

"Yes. I didn't understand it, but then I am not a cryptic person. I only saw the first episode and gave up."

"It wasn't everybody's taste, but I enjoyed it."

They made their way to the operating room and found Giles, a friendly and robust man. Nightingale always thought when he saw Giles that he would be more suited driving a tractor and running a farm, but his first love was working out the puzzles that the dead brought to him.

"Afternoon, gentlemen. Just in time. Now let's see what he can tell us."

The post mortem took a couple of hours and at the end of it, they knew that Simon Goodall was in very good health generally. He had a large amount of alcohol in his body. Giles took some blood for toxicology, but both Nightingale and Keane remembered that there were two empty wine bottles at the scene. The fingerprints on them and the accompanying glasses were being run through the computer that very afternoon. Giles took Goodall's fingerprints for them to put into the system when they got back. Then there was a surprise. Goodall suffered from eczema. Nightingale remembered that the Hendon Four (that name had stuck now) had all suffered from this condition. He had the remains of some sort of cream rubbed on it. It was located in his hair and the cream had made the hair greasy. Nightingale made a mental note to ask about the others. Was there any sign of a cream on their eczema?

Nightingale and Keane had a cup of tea with Giles after he had finished.

"What a puzzle, Richard. Let's see if toxicology can throw anything up."

"If he's like the others, it won't," said Keane, helping himself to a Bourbon biscuit.

"I think I'll go to Hendon tomorrow," said Nightingale. "Ferret around a bit. Talk to a few people."

"Do I get to come?" asked Keane. He was really getting fired up about this case. It was a long time since they'd had a murder, and one with such widespread implications was just up his street.

"Yes, you can come. Have you got anything better to do?"

"Not really, sir. This case seems to be taking up all our time, doesn't it? Besides I really would like to talk to the pathologist who carried out the four post mortems."

The two men finished their tea and polished off the biscuits, much to Giles' disappointment. He made a mental note to keep some back next time. They said their farewells and drove back to the station. Nightingale didn't entertain Keane with more singing or even a tape. They drove in silence most of the way and then Nightingale suddenly said:

"Do you know anything about untraceable poisons, Keane?"

Keane was surprised,

"No guv, 'fraid not. I suppose that's the way our minds should go."

"Yes, I'll have a discussion with Neville Lambert tomorrow when we get to Hendon."

When they reached the police station Ralph Beddows was waiting for them. He was with a tall and very elegant woman.

"Hello Ralph, sorry you had to wait."

"Don't worry, we haven't been here long. This is Laura Goodall, Simon's wife."

Nightingale shook her hand and said.

"We've just been to the morgue. Will you identify Simon for us, Mrs Goodall?"

"Yes. I'd like to see him. But what happened, Inspector? I really can't believe this has happened."

"We're trying to find out, Mrs Goodall. We believe it is related to four more murders in London recently. Do you know of anybody who would have wanted Simon dead? I can't believe that he had an enemy who felt that strongly, but you know him, can you think of anybody"

"No, not at all. We have some lovely friends and I can't think that any of them would want to kill him."

She started to weep. Silently, but tears ran down her cheeks.

"I'm sorry, Laura," said Ralph, and he ran his arm around her shoulders. "You don't have to do this today, you know. Tomorrow will do."

Nightingale felt a sudden compassion for this woman. He did not know her – yet. He expected he would learn more about her over the coming weeks.

"I want to do it today, if that's all right. I need to see him so that I will know he really is dead," replied the woman.

Nightingale could understand her thoughts, and he asked Keane to take her and Ralph to the morgue.

"I'll just phone them to let them know we are on the way" said Keane and disappeared through the inner door. Nightingale made small talk with Ralph until Keane's return.

"OK, shall we go?" he asked and the three of them left the station.

Nightingale made his way to Fisher's office, He sank into the chair and was enfolded by the wood panelling. It was hard to think there was a wicked world out there from his position opposite Fisher, but there certainly was. Fisher looked at a file on his desk.

"The only fingerprints we could identify on the bottles and glasses were Goodall's." He said, "There is another set, but they are not on the computer. We think it is a man from the size the hands would be."

"Really," replied Nightingale, "I'll ask Ralph Beddows and Mrs Goodall if they can think who it would be."

"Results on the dregs of wine in the bottles will be back tomorrow."

"Mrs Goodall is here," said Nightingale. "She's gone with Keane to officially identify her husband. She's a brave woman, sir. Would you like to meet her later?"

"Yes, yes I would, Richard. They have a son, I understand."

"Yes. I would imagine he's with Molly Beddows at the moment. I'll get a WPC to sit with them when she gets back from the morgue. I don't know where they are going to stay tonight, but I'll have a word with Ralph Beddows, if not with them then there must be a parishioner who will take them in."

"Good man, thanks Richard. Are you still going to Hendon tomorrow?"

"Yes, I thought we would. Simon's death has brought up a couple of new questions. My tame pathologist is a lovely man. He's meeting us there. I expect Mrs Goodall would appreciate a day to get herself more together, and to spend some time with their son."

"You're probably right," Fisher returned the evidence bag containing the note to Nightingale and rose from his chair. He walked to the window and gazed out to the car park. "You don't need me to tell you that it will be a considerable feather in our caps if we can solve these murders. I know that officially we only have one of our own, but we know they are connected and you are a very competent copper, Richard. Do you want more men?"

"Probably," replied Nightingale. "Can we have a meeting when I get back the day after tomorrow? Of course, I'm available all day tomorrow if you want me. You have all the telephone numbers where I'll be, just put a call through, I'd better go and see if I can find Laura Goodall."

Nightingale rose. "Anything else, sir?"

"Not that I can think of at the moment. At least I didn't have to suffer the conference today. See you later. Cheerio."

Nightingale found Keane with Laura Goodall in his office drinking tea.

"Hello, sir. We didn't think you'd mind."

"Not at all. How are you feeling, Mrs Goodall? It's devastating to have to identify a body. How are you bearing up?"

Laura Goodall's voice with thin and weak, "I'm not bad. It was nice to see him. He looked so peaceful, but I can't believe I'll never speak to him again or that we won't laugh together over something silly..." Her voice trailed off and silent tears ran down her cheeks.

Nightingale turned to Keane. "Where is the son?" Nightingale had been right, Molly Beddows had him and it had been arranged for them to stay at the vicarage for the night. Nightingale nodded to Keane on receiving this information.

"We'll take you back to the vicarage, if you're ready, Mrs Goodall," said Keane.

She nodded and said quietly, "Yes, I'd like to see Matthew. I've got to talk to him this evening about his Dad."

"Yes, I suppose you have. Would you like to WPC to be there?"

"No, thank you Sergeant. I must do this myself and alone. He's 14, I do hope he understands fully what I have to tell him"

"Come on then. Let's get you back to him."

Laura Goodall and Keane left the building and Nightingale fell deep into thought. He knew nothing at all about untraceable poisons, but this was something he would have to look into. He would speak to Neville Lambert tomorrow. He had arranged to meet him at the Hendon Morgue. He could return to the library but he doubted whether that kind of information was available to the man in the street. Yes, he would talk to Neville.

By the time Keane returned, Nightingale had got through all the biscuits, which peeved Keane slightly.

"So it's a good job I bought these," said Keane producing a package of Bourbons from his pocket.

"Where did you get those from?" Asked an amazed Nightingale. Keane had pulled a rabbit from his hat again.

"John's shop. Tracey and Karen were working today. The terrible twins."

"I love those two," said Nightingale. "They give everybody the impression that they don't take anything seriously, but they're right on the ball. No cheating or short change. They're great."

"Did you know that Karen's rabbit died? She loved that rabbit. It lived in the house and was her little baby. She tells me we've got a new vet in Market Langley. A lady vet. Have you come across her yet?"

"No, but Clare might have spoken to her. I'm sorry about Karen's rabbit. I would be devastated if anything happened to one of our cats, so I know how she feels. Is it time to go home yet Keane? We've got a long day tomorrow, we'd better get our beauty sleep. Come on, let's go. Tomorrow is another day."

They left their offices and went to the car park. There were only a handful of cars there and two of those were marked cars. Nightingale noticed that Fisher's car was missing and chuckled.

"What?" asked Keane.

"Oh, nothing. Have you ever noticed that the higher in rank a copper goes, the fewer hours he appears to work."

"Yes, I have," said Keane firmly. "I like being hands-on and I don't ever want to be more than an Inspector."

"We agree," replied Nightingale, "Now I'm a DCI, I have no ambition to go any higher and sit behind a desk all day."

"Hear, hear. Come on DCI Nightingale, let's go and see our women. See you in the morning at 7.30 at your house."

"OK. Good night, Tonto!" And they both drove home, each wondering what the next day would bring.

CHAPTER SIX

It was still dark when Nightingale got out of bed the next morning. He showered, shaved and dressed in the dark to avoid waking Clare. The cats were milling around his feet, determined to trip him up.

"Come on then, you lot. Let's see what I can find for you."

Bramble, Chutney and their three-legged rescue cat, Hops, all followed him to the kitchen. He put the lights on – what a relief – and went to their food cupboard. There was plenty of food there, enough for a banquet, thought Nightingale. The cats all lined up in the particular order that they were fed, and waited for Nightingale to fill their dishes. There was the sound of gentle purring as he placed the dishes in front of them, one by one. As they got on with their breakfast, Nightingale put the kettle on to boil and placed two slices of bread into the toaster. It was too early for the newspaper so he had to be satisfied with reading the narrative on the cat-food tins, His conclusion was that they probably ate better than a lot of people. He even thought that he wouldn't mind being a taster for cat food – in another life – it certainly smelled yummy.

His thought were broken by the clang of the toaster as the bread tried to escape out of the top. He decided to have marmalade on the toast and got down to eating it, when a dishevelled Clare appeared in the doorway.

"You couldn't make more noise if you tried!" she complained goodnaturedly. "What are you eating?"

"Toast," replied Nightingale.

The cats had finished their breakfast and were rubbing around Clare's ankles.

"Morning, boys. Have…?"

"Yes, and the kettle's about to boil. Would you like a cup of tea?"

"Oh, yes please."

Clare sat on a stool at the table while Nightingale made the drinks.

"I've got to take Hops to the vet today. It's time for his annual check-up and vaccination. Do you want to come?"

"I've got to go to north London today. I'd like to come. Can you make it tomorrow?"

"Yes, I'm sure I can. It will be an opportunity to meet the new vet, if I can get an appointment with her. I don't even know her name."

"No, neither do I. I only found out about her yesterday. It would be good to meet her."

"Right, consider it done. I'll change the appointment this morning."

The door bell rang.

"That'll be Keane. I'll let him in, I'm decent."

"Well I don't call thick pyjamas and a dressing gown being indecent. I'll make him a cup of tea."

Keane looked remarkably chipper for the early hour.

"Oh, tea. Thank you, Clare."

"How are you, David, I haven't seen you for a while."

"Ask the old man," replied Keane "He works me like a mule, don't you, sir?"

"You love it. We're on a jaunt today, but I hope it will be very productive. I'll introduce you to Neville Lambert. Make friends with him,

Keane, he will be very helpful in your future career. You never know when you'll need him."

Keane nodded as he sipped his hot tea.

"Will do, sir. We should get some really good information today."

"You're quite right Keane. Don't rush your tea, but we ought to get going soon."

Keane finished his tea and both men stood up. Nightingale ruffled Bramble's fur.

"Ta ta, old fellow. See you tonight."

He kissed Clare on the forehead and he and Keane headed for the front door, Nightingale still holding a piece of toast. They all said their goodbyes and the policemen got into Keane's car for the drive to Hendon. Keane did not keep music in his car, but he put the radio on. Radio 2 came as a welcome distraction for Nightingale, as he listened to the music played at that time of the day.

"Who are Bananarama then?" he asked.

"They're an all girls group, and not too bad," said Keane. "Do you like to listen to them sir?"

"Well, I heard one of the young chaps at the station mention them and thought you would know about them. Maybe I need to be educated in modern music, don't you think?"

"Well, it would take me longer than a trip to north London to tell you all you need to know, but if you really want to know, I'll bring a few tapes along in future and we can go through them. But do you really know nothing about modern music?"

"Not a thing Keane. Perhaps I ought to take the Learn Keanely course."

"OK, you're on. We'll start tomorrow"

Keane smiled to himself. He had never thought Nightingale liked modern music, and it turned out that he just knows nothing about it. He would enjoy teaching his boss the finer points of Culture Club.

The journey took about three hours, but they eventually pulled into the Hendon police station car park. The building was a modern edifice and they were taken to the canteen by a very dapper DCI who had been waiting for them. His name was Cooper and Nightingale thought he was the same shape as a wooden barrel, from which his name derived. Keane very quickly started making notes about the Hendon Four. Neville Lambert arrived just before lunchtime and was overjoyed to see them.

"Dickie, old chap how lovely to see you, and who's this, your sergeant?"

"Yes, David Keane." Keane shook hands with Lambert. "Well, just as long as you've got him under control, Keane. He can lose most of us with his intelligence. Don't let him baffle you by science."

Keane had never seen that side of Nightingale and wondered just what he was like when younger. Firstly, nearly everybody outside Market Langley called him Dickie Bird. Keane supposed he had a hidden past that was very different from the present day. Also, he seemed to know everybody in the Met. Keane thought that he must do some research about his kindly boss. He was intrigued by what sort of past he could have.

Nightingale, Keane and Lambert borrowed an office and Lambert proceeded to tell them what he had found. He seemed intrigued by the fact that they all suffered from eczema to varying degrees. Nightingale mentioned that Simon had obviously just put some cream of some sort on his eczema. When Lambert heard this he became excited.

"Yes, they all had some cream on their lesions." His report said it was 1% Hydrocortisone cream, the usual treatment for eczema. "I expect you will find your chap was using the same cream. The funny thing is that we could not find a half-used tube in his bathroom. Do let me know if you find any at your crime scene. There are lots of similarities between these cases and it's definitely the same perpetrator, but all the clues are very strange. Think about it, no cause of death, all had been drinking, the cream on the eczema, and, well, the eczema itself."

"Yes, Neville. It has more to it then we have found out at the moment. I say, would you like some lunch? We're a bit late but I'm sure we can find somewhere that will feed us."

"Not inside this building, you won't. At least not unless you want a floppy salad."

"No thanks. Do you know somewhere we can go?"

"Yes. Let's go to my house. Gwen will make us something and I know she'd love to see you."

"What a lovely idea. I haven't seen Gwen since I left London. Lead on, Macuff!"

Keane drove behind Lambert, following him to a very large bungalow on the outskirts of the town. On arrival, Lambert lead the way inside and called out: "Gwen, are you here? I've got a surprise for you."

Gwen appeared in a doorway. "Oh my word, Dickie! I haven't seen you for years. How lovely."

"Can you find us some lunch?" asked Lambert.

"I should think so. How about a ham omelette? I've got some fresh eggs from the chickens next door."

Neville nodded his head and Nightingale and Keane were very enthusiastic. "So be it," said Gwen "Our neighbours keep chickens, which are beautiful and the eggs are just wonderful. Dark golden yokes and really yummy. You go into the lounge and Neville will get you a drink, unless you'd prefer tea or coffee."

"Tea for me please" said Keane, "Driver, I'm afraid."

"What a shame. OK I'll get you a mug of tea. Come and make sure I do it right for you.'

Keane followed Gwen into the kitchen, and Neville poured two beers for himself and Nightingale.

"So, how's life in the countryside?" asked Neville "I expect it's a lot quieter there than it is around here."

"I would think so, but can you do something that I think was omitted from your investigation?"

"What's that, Dickie?"

"Could you check with all the victims' doctors if they were prescribed the cortisone cream? It's a prescription-only medicine, and there was none in any of the victims' houses."

"By George, I think you're on to something. If it was not prescribed where did it come from, and where did it go? And if it was prescribed, it's a bit of a coincidence that they all had it."

"What do you think about this eczema, Neville? If two of them had suffered from it, I would have been suspicious, but the fact that they all did, even our man in Sussex, is a bit too much to bear."

"Yes, I can only say that they must have been related to each other. Eczema runs in families, usually with asthma, but only one of the victims suffered from that, the rest just suffered the eczema. Leave it to me, Dickie, I'll see what I can find out tomorrow, or even this afternoon if the right people are available."

Gwen and Keane entered the room, Keane carrying his mug of tea.

"Hello, you two, putting the world to rights then?"

"Not all of it," said Neville, "just our corner of it."

"So, if it's ham omelette all round I'll get on with it," smiled Gwen and she left the three men to talk.

Lambert and Nightingale told Keane the contents of their last conversation and he seemed to be very excited by it.

"Do you really think they could all be related?" he asked.

"Well, it would be pretty amazing, but it's one option. And if they were related, they were all killed for Edward Gough, and we have to find out which one and why. This case gets more and more interesting as we go along."

Nightingale saw the excitement in Keane's face and continued:

"Of course, it does not make sense that four people in Hendon, who might be related to each other, are somehow related to our man in Market Langley, and the killer must have a wide range of contacts to find all the information he or she would need to track them all down. This needs a head-banging session when we get home." Keane laughed at the use of the phrase and once again had to admit to himself that Nightingale was streets ahead of most people in intelligence.

Gwen chose this moment to announce that the first omelette was ready and the next one was on its way. They all walked through to the kitchen and sat around the table. Keane could not wait to see what they could find out that afternoon.

CHAPTER SEVEN

The afternoon of that day was spent, by and large, hitting brick walls. The one thing they did find out was that the Cortisone cream was not prescribed by any of the doctors used by the Hendon Four. In fact, the victims had not even reported the eczema to their doctors. This was so strange that for the rest of the afternoon Nightingale was deep in thought as to what this information could mean. He was not really concentrating on Neville and Keane, but thinking back over the centuries, wondering how they treated eczema in the 1700s, and if they even knew what it was. Finally, he shook these thoughts away from him and bid a grateful farewell to Neville making a mental note to send Gwen some flowers. Keane drove them back to Market Langley and wondered how on earth he was going to introduce the music Nightingale suddenly seemed interested in to a man who was steeped in opera. He decided to start with Duran Duran the next day. He would leave Wham for later.

When they got home, they parted at Nightingale's house and both men were lost in thought. They would, indeed, have to have a head-banging session tomorrow, Clare had managed to get an afternoon appointment at the vet's for Hops. Nightingale looked forward to going to the vet's, the vets and nurses were so dedicated to the animals. Nightingale thought: "It's a pity that people in other walks to life don't have the same dedication."

Keane was at home listening to June's account of her day. He needed something like this to clear his head and allow him to sleep. He joined in the conversation about the parking problem in town and gradually began to wind down.

Both men were at the police station by 8 o'clock the next day. Nightingale wrote himself a very large note on a piece of A4 paper reminding him to leave at 2.30. The appointment at Bonnies, the vet's was at 3.30, and he didn't want to be late, He blue-tacked the note to the glass on the door to the room, much to Keane's amusement.

Nightingale sat at his desk and motioned Keane to sit down.

"We've got a lot to think about. How do you fancy that head-banging session?"

"Let me get two cuppas and some biscuits and I think we'll be ready," replied Keane.

Ten minutes later, Keane was armed with Garibaldi biscuits and tea and sat down.

"Oh, good, Dead Fly biscuits!" smiled Nightingale.

"You've put me right off them now. They do look like squashed flies, don't they?"

"Pretend I didn't say anything." smiled Nightingale, "They really are scrummy."

"Yes, I'll try and keep squashed flies out of my mind." Keane did not say anything more about it, but Nightingale noticed that he did not eat a biscuit.

The two men went over the case as they had the details so far. It seemed odd to both men that if the murders were carried out for some reason related to Edward Gough that there were four in Hendon and only one locally, especially when they had established that both men called Edward Gough lived locally. Of course, they still did not know the method of murder, but Nightingale had not forgotten that there might be a link to untraceable poison of some kind. And where, oh where, did the eczema fit in, together with the lack of hydrocortisone cream in the victims' homes?

Nightingale suddenly said, "How do you fancy a trip to Hendon again, and this time go to the parish church and the library to see if you can find anything about Ertol and Edward Gough thereabouts? Also could you see if there are any references to a woman called Patience and her husband Jez Waters together with their children and what became of them all. I've got to go back to the library and see if I can find a link between Edward Gough and Simon Goodall. I know it's all tenuous, but we've got to find some links."

"Where did all that come from, sir?" asked Keane

"It's been churning around in my mind since yesterday, and it's come to the surface because I'm a DCI and you're a DS. When you can think like that you'll be a DCI too." Nightingale patted Keane on the back and ate the last Garibaldi biscuit.

"I'll get some chocolate ones in future." Sighed Keane. He really liked Garibaldi biscuits but he probably would never touch another one in his life. Every time he thought of them, he thought of squashed flies.

"Am I going to Hendon tomorrow, then?" asked Keane.

"I think so," replied Nightingale. "We really have to write up what we've got for the old man. I'll tell you what, you write it up this afternoon. I'll be back about 4.30 or so and I can go over it. I don't see why we can't present your report to Fisher. How do you feel about that?"

"Thank you, sir. I'd really appreciate that. I'll get on to it after lunch."

"Right oh. I'll buy you lunch at the Lamb, they always do good food there. We've been head-banging for four hours, where does the time go?"

"Don't know sir, but I'd appreciate lunch, I'm a bit hungry." And he picked up the empty biscuit packet and threw it into the bin.

"Sorry, old chap. I won't do it to you again," said Nightingale, feeling truly sorry that he had brought up the subject of flies at all.

As they walked along the road in the direction of the pub, Keane said: "I'm sorry I can't bring you the delights of my music selection today, sir, but we just haven't been out in the car."

"Never kind, Keane. I'm sure there will be plenty of opportunity to rectify the situation. I really am looking forward to finding out what the youngsters listen to. I tried putting the radio on in the car this morning and I really must say, I like Wham! Are they good looking? I bet they are. Nobody ever became famous by being ugly."

Keane laughed, "I beg to differ. What about Marty Feldman?"

"Yes, I suppose he is the exception that that proves the rule. Have you ever seen a picture of his wife? She's absolutely beautiful."

"Yes, I have seen a picture of her. It's amazing that she should have been attracted to him."

"We'll never know why. Ah, here we are. After you David. I'm in the chair, what would you like to drink?"

The two men vanished into the smoky depths of the pub and soon had two pints of local beer and a portion of shepherd's pie each. They spent a happy hour chatting about Wham! and Duran Duran. Nightingale really was keen to hear some of their music. After all he should keep up with the things youngsters listened to and he liked what he was hearing. He made a mental note of watch Top of the Pops that week. He thought that he would be shaken by what he saw, but he had to try it out.

When the two men arrived back at the police station, Nightingale looked at his watch.

"Must go Keane, time and tide wait for no man. I'm off to the vet's."

"OK sir. Are you coming back later?"

"Yes, I hope so. If I'm not going to make it back I'll ring you."

"Righty oh. See you later." And the two men parted, Keane back to write his report for Fisher and Nightingale into his car. He hesitated about playing a tape and turned the radio on instead. The presenter announced "a blast from the past" and played Come on Eileen by Dexy's Midnight Runners. Nightingale found his hands tapping on the steering wheel and his head moving from side to side with the music. He was somewhat amazed to find out at the end of the record that it was released in 1983. He could see that he had a lot of back numbers to listen to as well as the present music.

When he arrived home Clare had Hops in his basket and was ready to go. They both got into the car and put Hops on the back seat. As they drove into Market Langley Nightingale said

"Have you ever heard of Dexy's Midnight Runners love?"

"Of course I have, they're a part of my youth. Why do you ask?"

"I've just discovered them. Keane is trying to bring me up to date with music and I must say I really enjoyed Come On Eileen."

Clare smiled. "I never thought I'd hear you say something like that. How far back are you going? I've got a box of tapes in the loft, I'll get them out tomorrow and we can go through them."

"That would be terrific" said Nightingale "Ah, here we are. I'll carry Hops, he's getting heavy these days."

They walked across the car park at the front of the vet's surgery. The receptionist greeted them well and made Nightingale smile to himself when she said "Is this Hops Nightingale?"

"Yes," replied Clare, "Check-up and jabs today."

"Take a seat and I'll tell Nancy you're here."

After a short wait, during which Hops tried to shout the place down, Nancy Dean appeared and called them into the consulting room.

"We haven't got another cat called Hops on our register, but don't think we've got another three-legged cat either. I've just looked at his history, and he's four years old, isn't he?"

"That's right," said Clare. "I hope he didn't disturb anybody with his constant yelling."

"No, don't worry. Would you mind if one of our nurses sits in on our consultation. Sean is our head nurse and he wants to see how a cat can manage with three legs."

"Not at all," said Nightingale, "The more the merrier."

Nancy picked up the intercom in the consulting room and asked for Sean to come in. He was a very pleasant-looking young man with dark auburn hair and brown eyes.

"Hello, Sean," said Clare. "We understand you're interested in Hops."

"Yes, very. Are you sure you don't mind my being here?"

Nightingale smiled at him "We carrot tops must stick together."

Everybody laughed, and Nancy said: "I am really finding the patients and owners here to be an absolute delight."

"It must be a bit different from, where was it? Twickenham?" smiled Clare.

"Oh yes, totally."

"What about you, Sean? I haven't seen you before either." Clare turned to look at him and was delighted to see that he winked at her.

"Yes, I've only been here three weeks and I'm loving it already. I came from Hemel Hempstead, and nothing could be more different."

They spent five minutes learning about Hemel Hempstead and then Nancy said "I think we'd better tend to Hops, he's getting restless."

"But at least he's stopped all that yodelling," said Clare as she took Hops out of his basket. The examination went well. He was given a clear bill of health and Sean examined the old scar of his removed back leg. He commented that it was a lovely piece of surgery, and asked how it happened.

"We're not really sure, but he was hit by a car we think and the leg shattered so it had to come off. We took him from Cats Protection and he's been a delight to us ever since. He can run, jump and climb, but we'll have to be gentle with him when he gets older." Clare was stroking Hops as she spoke and he was completely docile.

"Right let's give him his jab and you can go. Yes, he will have to be watched when he gets older, but if he is cared for as he is now it shouldn't be too much trouble."

Nightingale took Hops to the pharmacy where the till was and paid the bill. Clare was still talking to Nancy and Sean and Nightingale had to tear her away.

"Well, what a lovely vet, and their head nurse seems to be charming," said Clare as they stowed Hops in the back seat of the car.

"Yes, and don't think I didn't see him wink at you," chuckled Nightingale. It was a constant source of delight to him to know that he had a wife whom other men found attractive. Clare's face coloured and she was glad that Nightingale was laughing.

"I didn't do it on purpose," she said.

"I know, darling," answered Nightingale, and he took her hand. "I find it flattering when men find you attractive."

"Well, thank goodness for that." said Clare, and the policeman drove her home.

When they arrived, Hops was greeted with suspicion by the other two cats. They could always smell the vet's surgery on each other and Hops settled down for a long washing session before he alienated Bramble and Chutney altogether.

"Have you got time for a coffee?" asked Clare. Nightingale looked at his watch, it was 4.45. "No thanks love, all that chatting has meant that I've got to go straight back to work."

Clare was disappointed, but said: "OK darling, see you later."

Nightingale went straight to the police station – with the radio on – and was enthralled by Bonnie Tyler singing Holding Out for a Hero. He loved it. He must find out when it was released and if he could get a copy.

He arrived at the police station humming the song and trying to remember the words. He found on entering his office, that Keane had written his report for Fisher and put it on Nightingale's desk. Nightingale read it immediately and found it to be excellent. "I won't have Keane for long," thought Nightingale. "He'll be an inspector before I know it." He took the report straight to Superintendent Fisher, who was in his office. He looked worried.

"Glad to see you, Nightingale. We have a problem."

"Nightingale sat down in the chair Fisher indicated. "What's up?" he asked.

"I've had a reporter from the Daily Mirror on the phone, asking about the murder of Goodall. I don't know how he found out, but we've got to try and keep this case a bit quiet. For one thing, we don't want reporters camping outside his house with Mrs Goodall and their son there, and we don't want the Hendon connection to be made; it would frighten some of their readers and would put the whole case in the public domain. I can see if it did get out that it would be all over the news on television and that would call for one of us to make a public statement." Fisher gave a sharp intake of breathe, "We don't want all this unsolicited attention, now do we?"

Nightingale frowned.

"We certainly don't. I suppose we shall never find out how they got wind of it, but I think I'll pay a visit to Mrs Goodall. I'll see how she is and let her know that we are releasing Simon's body for burial. I've brought you a report, this one written by Keane. It's good. See what you think and I'll see you in the morning after my visit to West Downfold."

"OK," replied Fisher, "Keane is coming along nicely. I think he'll be promoted soon, don't you?"

'That's what I'm afraid of. I don't want to lose him yet. I must admit he's an asset to have on the team. He's going to Hendon tomorrow. I've sent him on his own, so we shall see what he brings back."

"Excellent!" Fisher was impressed. "Just the sort of thing he needs - it will give him a real test. Off you go and see Mrs Goodall, and I'll see you in the morning."

Nightingale was quite proud of Keane and it was a fact that he wouldn't remain a sergeant for ever. Nightingale smiled and thought: "Now I've given him a phobia about Garibaldi biscuits, will he ever be the same again?"

Nightingale rang Mrs Goodall, but got no reply so he rang the Beddows' home. Molly answered.

"Yes, Laura's here. She's trying to escape the reporters that continually phone her. She has to unplug the phone at night to get some peace, poor dear."

"Can I come over to see her?" asked the policeman. "And I may be able to do something about the phone calls."

"Yes, come straight away," replied Molly "She'll be glad to see you."

Nightingale was not expecting a reception crowd, but the reporters had gathered outside the police station. They did not know who he was so he walked through the group unstopped. He knew they would have to make a statement the next day. When he got to his car, he phoned Fisher from the car phone and told him to look out of the window. Fisher was furious.

"Can you make a statement tomorrow, sir?"

"Yes, I'll have to. Did you speak to any of them?"

"No, sir. I just walked straight out."

"Good. I'll put something together and go to see them."

Nightingale rounded up Keane and they walked straight through the crowd of reporters to their car. They did not say a word to each other, nor to the reporters. The reporters did not know who they were, so they just let them pass.

"That's good," thought Nightingale. "At least we can get out of our own station."

They got in the car and headed off to the vicarage. They knew that Laura Goodall was staying there with her son. The reporters had made it impossible for them to live in their own home. It was such a shame, she was such a brave woman and now to be sought after by the collected press of the world seemed to be somewhat unfair to Nightingale, but he knew what they were like. They needed a story - it was their job and in their blood, and they would go to almost any lengths to get it. When they got to the vicarage Molly answered the door.

"Hello, you two," she said. "Have you come for something to eat again?"

"Hello, Molly, it's good to see you more cheerful," said Nightingale. "We've come to see Laura Goodall."

"Yes. You'd better come in. There aren't any reporters here but they're all around Laura's cottage."

"I'll get some policemen out there," said Nightingale. "They've started to gather at the police station as well. If we can get a few uniforms in position we can soon sort them out, I think."

Molly made them a cup of coffee and they sat with Laura Goodall in the tidy lounge at the vicarage. She seemed a lot braver than she had before. She was a strong woman anyway but she had to be strong now for Matthew. She hadn't let him see her cry and she had told him what a wonderful man his father was and he would believe that for the rest of his life. It was true Simon had been a good man and father. It was such a shame that this murderer had chosen him, but why had they chosen him? That was yet to be discovered, and Nightingale would move heaven and earth to make sure he found out.

Nightingale told Laura very gently that she could now bury Simon. The body had been released.

Matthew had been a patient boy. He knew his mother had been crying, he had seen his friends crying, Molly particularly. Molly had been devastated as Nightingale and Keane knew, but she had stopped her tears now and was a very strong back-up for Laura and Matthew. Matthew was as brave as his mother. Nightingale considered that maybe at the funeral was when Matthew would break down and that's when he would need his mother. Laura was thankful that they could now bury Simon, and made quick arrangements for Molly to take her into town to go to a funeral director. Nightingale and Keane left the vicarage feeling as if they had a job well done by supporting Laura and Molly as much as they could. Nightingale wondered if he ought to get a Victim Support officer to help her. He would ask her if she wanted one next time he saw her.

They got in the car and headed back to the station.

"Listen to this," said Keane. "I've selected a group called Duran Duran for you to listen to. I hope you like them." He played Rio on the car tape recorder. Now Nightingale thought this was great. He hadn't realised what he had been missing. He loved his opera and would always love his opera, but this new style he was discovering made his life just a little bit happier. He started to hum along with the tune and tapping his feet while Keane drove back to the police station. When they got there the press had gone. Fisher had made a statement in their absence and that had satisfied the press but no doubt they would be back tomorrow.

They went inside. Keane did his last rounds and joined Nightingale. The next day Keane would be going to Hendon and Nightingale would be trawling the public library for parish records. They hoped that this would bring them closer to the perpetrator of this crime who was a very clever person but still very much a mystery to them.

Nightingale arranged for several uniformed police officers to attend at the Goodall cottage to protect Laura and Matthew. He then phoned the vicarage. Molly and Laura were back from Market Langley and he informed them that the police officers should be at the cottage in the next half hour. He advised that Laura could go home if she wanted to and would be safe from the press. He suggested that she unplugged the phone for the night because the reporters would keep on ringing now they had her number.

That done, Nightingale headed off to Clare and the cats to spend what he hoped would be a very pleasant evening and he would introduce Clare to some of the songs Keane had been playing for him. He probably didn't need to, he knew that Clare knew all about Bonnie Tyler and Duran Duran.

When he got home Clare was out. He wondered where she'd gone. He fed the cats. All three were present and correct. Clare came in 10 minutes later and said,

"Oh, hello. I didn't know you'd be home. I've just been down to see Laura Goodall."

"I didn't know you knew her."

"Well, I do vaguely, but not very well. I thought she might need some comfort and she was very pleased to see me."

"So, my wife's a social caller now is she?" laughed Nightingale.

"Well, anything I can do for Laura. She's so lovely. I didn't know Simon but I taught Matthew and that's how I know them both."

"OK, love, let's have something to eat and a quiet evening in the company of Duran Duran."

CHAPTER EIGHT

When Nightingale drove into the police station the next morning, the press were still very much in evidence, although there were not as many now. Nightingale put this down to the fact that their story was not as topical any more, and they were not as interested as they had been. He walked straight through them and into the building where Fisher was already in his office. Nightingale knocked on the door and went in.

"Hello sir" he said, "I think we've got to do something about these reporters."

"Yes, I spoke to them yesterday," said Fisher. "But it doesn't seem have made them go away. I'll tell you what, we'll have a news conference, invite the news people. You can do the talking, I'll be there in support. We'll see if we can get Mrs Goodall to come and sit with us. She doesn't have to say anything, but I think it would be good if she is there. We should get them off our backs for quite a while."

"What a good idea," said Nightingale. "Get the press people to write something. I'll be back after lunch, and maybe we can sort something out for that time."

"OK," said Fisher, "let me get on to the press office and I'll let you know what they come up with this afternoon."

Meanwhile, Keane had left his house quite as early as Nightingale and was half way to Hendon. He'd skimped on breakfast and was feeling very hungry, but he knew that when he got there, the Hendon Nick canteen served a very good full breakfast, so he was not particularly concerned about his stomach feeling hollow. He was glad that Nightingale had given him the chance to do something on his own. He really did hope that he would make inspector before very long. He would miss Nightingale if he was taken away from him to work somewhere else in the country but he thought the time was almost right for him to become what he called "a grown up" and act on his own.

Nightingale thought that there was no point trying to telephone Laura Goodall as she was probably not answering the phone. He drove over to see her. He explained to her what Fisher's idea was and she was all for it. She said that she did not want to speak, but she would certainly like to be there if it would help find the person who had killed her husband. Nightingale left her and went back to the Parish Office, which was just on the outskirts of Marker Langley in the Council Office. They did not have a town hall at

Market Langley but they did have the large Council Office: a red brick building, very modern and out of keeping with most of the buildings in Market Langley.

Nightingale went inside and made his plea. He was looking for parish records from 1801 to 1950 when Simon Goodall was born. That's what he hoped Keane was doing in Hendon, so between them they should be able to make a double-sided attack on two towns that might have something to be with the death of Edward Gough.

Nightingale was shown by a very pretty young girl into the part of the Library of old documents. Again everything was on microfilm. They had parish records for Saints Peter and Paul going back to 1800, so the death of Edward in 1801 was just inside that parameter. He spent a happy hour going through the documents and getting copies of those he needed. By the end of the hour he had found a copy of Edward's death certificate. He had found birth certificates for the three girls who were children of Edward Senior and Louisa. He already had the link between the Goughs and the Goodalls. He hoped he would find the marriage certificate for Edward Snr. and Louisa but he had no luck there. He thought he would come back another day as it was not important if they were married or not but had discovered that there was Edward and Louisa, the parents of the three girls. He paid for his copies and left the building feeling quite elated. He wondered how Keane was getting on. He was very happy to send his Sergeant out on his own. It was almost time for him to become an Inspector as Keane knew and Nightingale was going to miss him when it happened, but it hadn't yet and there was still some training left to do.

Nightingale made his way back to the police station to pore over his finds to see what he could glean from them. Meanwhile, Keane had arrived in Hendon. He had made his way to the police station and caught up with Inspector Cooper.

"What, no Dickie today?" asked Cooper.

"No, he's let me out on my own. God knows what he thinks I'm going to do, but he's trusted me to come all this way on my own to gather some information, so I was wondering if you could help me."

"Of course, old boy," said Cooper. "What are you looking for?"

Keane explained that he was looking for parish records from 1801 to 1950. Cooper told him he would have to go to the Library where the parish records were kept. Keane then asked if the canteen was still serving breakfast.

"All day, old chap," said Cooper. "Come on, I'll come with you."

They went to the canteen and Keane ate a hearty breakfast.

"You're not a condemned man surely," said Cooper.

"What?" replied Keane

"You've eaten enough to last you for about a week!"

"Ah, yes, but I love fried breakfasts."

"You're going to have to watch that," said Cooper. "As you get older you'll get fatter. What will the ladies think of you then?"

"Ah, I've got my lady," said Keane. "She loves me what ever I look like"

"Glad to hear it" said Cooper. "Come on I'll take you over to the Council Offices."

They walked to the Council Offices from the police station. It was a newish building in a town of new buildings. Cooper made their request at reception, and they were taken to a room full of microfilm. He and Cooper spent two hours looking through the files. They found the Jez Waters whom Patience had married. He and Patience - the sister of Constance, the mother of Edward Jr. - had lived in Hendon all their married lives. They also found that Verity, one of the daughters of Edward Snr and Louisa, married the landlord of The White Bear public house and moved there in 1818. They must have had children, but Keane could find no reference to this. He did find that Patience had a brother, George. Simon Goodall was a direct descendant of Edward Snr and Louisa. So this was the link he had found between Hendon and the parish of Saints Peter and Paul in West Downfold. Keane was absolutely thrilled with this and paid for his copies. He thought he'd go back to the police station and phone Nightingale to let him know what they had found.

The two policemen walked back to the police station. It was quite a pleasant day.

"How old is your police station?" asked Keane

"Oh, it's only about 30 years old," replied Cooper. "We were in what served as a police station but was little more than a prefab before that. We're very glad to have this one now."

"Can you remember when it was a prefab?" asked Keane.

"Oh yes, I was just a beat copper then, but we've been happy here since then. I don't think they're going to move us again. We'll probably have to stay here until this one falls down."

Keane and Cooper laughed.

"Well, let's hope it's not soon," replied Keane, and the two men entered the police station.

"I must just phone Nightingale," said Keane.

"Give Dickie my best," said Cooper. "I'll meet you in the canteen for a cuppa when you've spoken to him."

Keane managed to catch Nightingale in between appointments. He'd just come back from the Council Offices and both men were thrilled by what they had found. Nightingale had traced a link between Patience and Simon Goodall. The line went directly from Patience to Goodall. The Goodalls had been living in Market Langley and West Downfold since 1805, so there was a very strong link there.

Keane was very busy telling Nightingale what he had found about the people in Hendon. Nightingale then said to him: "See if you can anything relating to the girls. What were their names?"

"Oh, I wrote them down. They were Verity, Florence and Dorcas."

"Good old names," said Nightingale. "See if you can find anything about them. If you do it now, it'll save us a journey later on."

"OK, sir." Said Keane, "I'll pop over there after lunch and then I'll come home."

"OK. Take care, my boy. See you tomorrow morning."

Nightingale hung up and thought to himself what a good man Keane was. He knew he could trust him to do this job.
He went back to his office to paw over the records he had found. The link with the Goodall family and Gough family was very plain once he'd seen the records. He was very pleased he had made that link, but where that took him he wasn't sure. He thought that the victims in Hendon and Simon were all related to Patience. It would be terrific if they were all related and he could find a motive for the murders. He carefully put the documents away in his drawer and went to see Fisher. The time set for the press conference was creeping up and he wanted to go through what the press office had written before he had to say it.

"I think you'd better pop off and get Mrs Goodall," said Fisher. "We can't expect her to bring herself into the station today and she probably doesn't feel like driving. She'd probably go into the back of the first car that stopped in front of her."

"Good idea sir," said Nightingale "I'll go and fetch her as soon as I've read through this brief."

He took the draft of what he had to say to his office and read it through. It all made sense without giving too much away to the public, and he thought how nice it would be to have Mrs Goodall there to back them up. No doubt the press would want to ask her questions but it would he who had to field them. He drove out to West Downfold and collected Mrs Goodall. She did not bring Matthew with her; they took him to the vicarage to stay with Molly whilst his mother was out.

"You'll see us on the six o'clock news," said Nightingale to Matthew, who found it very exciting that Mum was going to be on television. He didn't quite get the fact that it was because his father had been murdered, but little boys are little boys and he would soon grow up.

Nightingale arrived at the police station with Laura Goodall just as the mass of press were sorting themselves out. The press conference went very well: Nightingale straight faced and serious, and putting his point across. Laura Goodall managed to make her way through the press conference without crying which was a blessing. He then took her home and spent some time talking to Matthew, who just couldn't wait for the six o'clock news to see if he could see his mum on television. Young boys are strange creatures, but they soon grow up and Nightingale did not want to see Matthew grow up too soon.

Keane made his way back from Hendon, and it seemed the day was over. He had the information he needed, tracing Verity to the White Bear. They had been very good to him at Hendon and Cooper had been remarkably nice to him. Mind you, all the policemen in far-flung places that Nightingale knew were really nice to him and to Keane. It made Keane think that Nightingale must have done something or been the sort of copper that everybody liked when he was in the Met and surrounding areas. He was going to find out why, he had no idea how but find out he would.

Keane had discovered that Verity Gough had married the publican of the White Bear in Hendon so she was placed there, while the rest of her family were placed at West Downfold. He also discovered that Jez Waters, who had married Patience, the aunt of Gough Jnr also moved to Hendon. So he had both families with representatives in Hendon and West Downfold.

Now where that would lead he was not quite sure at the moment, but he and Nightingale would have what Nightingale called a head-banging session the next day to see if they could find out any more about the relationship between the two families.

Keane arrived home slightly earlier than normal. June was delighted to see him and they had a pleasant hour sitting in the garden drinking a glass of wine before they had their evening meal. Keane knew he was never find another boss as good as Nightingale. Although it was on the cards that he would become an Inspector soon, he did not want it to come too soon because he would miss his close relationship with Nightingale and his guiding hand.

Nightingale, meanwhile, had also gone home. All the cats lined up in the kitchen in their usual places while he fed them. Clare arrived a quarter of an hour later. The two of them sat and drank a glass of wine before dinner. It was so nice for both policemen to be home slightly early, even though they were tired out, both of them knew that they had made some ground on their enquiry, but neither of them knew where it would lead them. They had a lot of information now, but where it was going to take them they did not know. They knew they had to find somebody with a relationship to either the Gough family, the Greene family or the Waters family, or maybe even to all three. But find it they would if it took them the rest of the year; they would solve this case. They both knew that they had to solve it to give themselves peace of mind again before anybody else was murdered. That is the thought that they took to bed with them that night.

Chapter Nine

Nightingale popped his head round Keane's door: "My office, ten Minutes and bring the biscuits." He then vanished.

Keane smiled to himself. Nightingale had a way with him that charmed everybody, even the men he worked with. Keane had managed to save half a packet of chocolate bourbons and had a packet of chocolate-covered biscuits. Now, should he take them both to the meeting or not? He decided in the end that he should, so he made his way along the corridor holding two packets of biscuits and a file. Anyone seeing him would have thought he was the tea boy.

Nightingale was waiting for him when he entered the office.

"Ah, chocolate biscuits – lovely. Let's make a cup of tea and get our heads round what problems we've got and have a head-banging session. I think we've done very well to find the traces of three families in both places, but we've got to see if we can pin down more members of the Greene family. Or for that matter, the Waters family. Let's put the kettle on and we'll start to think. What we really need to do," said Nightingale turning away from the kettle, "what we really need to do is to find out if any of the Hendon Four were related to the Greene, Waters or Gough families. I think this is a family feud you know, taken out of all proportion by somebody very ruthless, and probably very ill."

"Yes, sir," said Keane, "I was beginning to think that. We don't need to go to Hendon again. I can phone the parish records office from here and see if we can find any other relations of all the families, up to the present day. We know that Simon Goodall was a relative of the Greenes so maybe that's something we should think about."

"I agree," said Nightingale. "By Jove, we are clever, aren't we?"

Keane laughed: "Here you are sir, have a biscuit and calm down."

"Yes, maybe I should. By the way. I heard a group called Blondie on the way into work today. Sounded great. Someone called Debbie Harry singing. I'd really like to hear more of their stuff. Mind you there are a lot of people I'd like to hear more of. You've really got me going now with music from the 80s."

"Good," said Keane. "Maybe you should listen to my record collection. I can lend you some of my tapes."

"That would be excellent. Thank you. Finish your biscuit, have your cup of tea and then go back and phone Hendon if you would. See if we can find any relations in the present for the Greenes, Waters or Goughs. I think that's the way to go, don't you?"

"Absolutely right, sir. Aren't you clever? Now I know why I'm still a Sergeant."

"No., it runs in the family, didn't you know?"

"Family?" said Keane, "Don't tell me you think we're related now."

"You know what I mean, our police family here at the station. We're the cleverest in the country sometimes. We've managed to unearth some of the answers to this problem when everybody else had failed, so I think we can give ourselves a pat on the back."

"Thank you sir. I'll finish my biscuit with relish and then I'll get on the phone."

"What's your opinion on my feud idea? Do you think it's possible?"

"Well, it did cross my mind, but I thought it would have been a long time ago and too long for someone to hold a grudge about something that happened before they were born."

"Right," said Nightingale, "but we both know that criminals are often a sandwich short of a picnic."

Keane smiled. Nightingale had a way with words that summed things up with as few words as possible.

"We found that out in 1987. Do you remember?"

"I do Keane, but at least we know that the perpetrator is behind bars for the rest of his life."

"Do you keep in touch with the Saunders? Did you say they had a baby now?"

"Yes. I know it's a little girl, but she must be about two now. I'll make a point of visiting them this week, just to catch up. Sally Saunders, the wife, was very ill after that case."

"I remember. But then she did blame herself for her children's deaths. It must have been awful for her."

"She had the best treatment, and I'm sure the new baby is a delight for her."

"When you go, give them my best, won't you, sir?"

"Of course, Keane, but back to the present. I think we ought to compile family trees for the Greenes, the Waters and the Goughs. It will be a pain and time consuming but I think that's the only way forward. We must find the living relatives of all the players."

"Well, I'll make a start on the Hendon end. Do you want to take West Downfold or would you like me to do that as well?"

"I'll do West Downfold," said Nightingale. "I've got a mole at the library who will gladly help."

Again Keane smiled. What a super boss he had. He finished his biscuit and went back to his desk to make a start by phoning Hendon.

Before he rang the parish office, Keane put a call through to Cooper at the police station.

"Hello David, this is Cooper the Copper, you wanted to talk to me."

"Yes. I hope you don't mind my poking me nose in, but it seems to me that my DCI gets respect and friendship from every copper he meets, is there a reason for that?"

"I'm surprised you don't know David, but he never was one for blowing his own trumpet."

"Oh, tell me, do."

"In 1980, when Richard was a lowly beat copper in the Met, he answered a radio call from a copper in trouble. When he got there, there was a scallywag with a gun held on PC Carter. He talked to the man and disarmed him. He got the Queen's Gallantry Medal."

"Wow. I would never have guessed. We met Ian Carter during a case in '87 and something was mentioned, but the Queen's Gallantry Medal, that's terrific."

"Don't you go telling him I mentioned it to you. He might never speak to me again!"

"No, I won't dob you in, but thanks for telling me. I'll hold him in great respect from now on. How super."

"Yes, he's a brilliant copper now, and gets respect from everybody who knows him. We're all up for helping him whenever we can."

"Thank you again. You never know, I might see you soon."

"Cheerio, old chap. Nice to speak to you."

Keane had a huge smile on his face as he phoned the parish office. He was put through to a very helpful young lady who seemed to know her way around the births and deaths very well. She found the death certificates for the Hendon Four and worked backwards. Within 20 minutes Keane had written down the names of all their relatives living, and in had discovered that the early 1800s all four families were connected by marriage. Keane could not believe his ears. This was just what they wanted. The young woman printed off all the relevant copies and said they would be in the post that evening. Keane just sat at his desk with a stupid grin on his face. He had found what they had suspected, but now they had concrete proof. He shook himself and took his piece of paper along the corridor to Nightingale.

Nightingale was getting his things together for a trip to see Laura Goodall. He had the phone in his hand and was talking into it.

"OK, meet you at the vicarage in half an hour. Bye bye."

He replaced the handset and looked at Keane.

"You're going to tell me you found the link, aren't you?"

"Yes, sir. These are all the names" He handed Nightingale his piece of paper. "And I think that the vet, Nancy Dean, is one of the relatives of the Gough family. We ought to check it out thoroughly and warn her."

"Really?" Nightingale looked very serious, "Yes, when are you going to get the copies?"

"They should be here tomorrow. Where are you going?"

"I'm meeting Laura Goodall at the vicarage with Ralph and Molly Beddows, they want to talk to me. Get your jacket, Keane, you're coming too."

They drove to West Downfold in glorious sunshine. Nightingale turned the radio on and found they were playing "Heart of Glass" by Blondie. He hummed along to it and then when it had finished, he said to Keane:

"That girl has a lovely voice. Is she pretty?"

"Not pretty, guv, beautiful. She's blonde, of course, and a bit moody."

"I don't know if I like moody people Keane, but I'd have to see her I suppose. I watched Top of the Pops this week. What a culture shock! But I'll stay with it, I just like the music."

"I never thought I'd hear you say that. Have you heard Love Cats, by the Cure?"

"No, will I like it?"

"You'll like the song and I don't know whether you will like The Cure to look at. They're very strange."

"You must let me hear it, anything about cats will be my cup of tea. I don't have to look at them do I?"

"No guv. I'll bring along a tape tomorrow."

"Good man." said Nightingale as they pulled into the front of the vicarage. Ralph, Molly and Laura were waiting for them. They were sitting under the tree in the garden drinking iced tea. Keane had to make an effort to remember why they were there. The scene looked very tranquil and he had to force himself to remember that they were there because of a murder.

"Hello, everybody," said Nightingale. "How are you, Mrs Goodall?"

"Not too bad," she replied, "Now I've got the funeral arranged things seem a bit better."

"That's what we wanted to speak to you about," said Ralph. "We wondered if you would like to say a few words on the day? I'll be doing the eulogy, but maybe you can think of something."

"Well, my favourite poem for these occasions has always been that one that goes 'I've just slipped into another room' - do you know it? I don't know who wrote it, but I could read that."

"That would be good, but Laura has a poem that was read at their wedding that she'd rather like read. Elizabeth Barrett-Browning, Sonnet from the Portuguese. It's a strange title but I'm sure you know it. It starts 'How do I love thee, let me count the ways?'."

"I know it" said Nightingale "If I explain that it was read at their wedding, I'm sure it will be lovely. Yes, I'd be glad to do it."

"Thank you, Richard," said Laura, taking his hand. "I really want this to be a remembrance of Simon's life, and you are so tied up with it that I'm so glad you will do it."

Her eyes misted over and she dropped her head. Molly quickly said "I've made a cake, would you all like some?"

There was a chorus of Yes pleases. "Come on Laura, let's get the cake and some more tea."

Molly and Laura left the garden and headed towards the kitchen.

"How is she really?" asked Nightingale.

"Well, she's devastated but she's being very brave."

"When is the funeral?"

"Next Monday at 11.30. I'm having the grave dug on Saturday. Laura wanted somewhere to visit, she didn't want a cremation."

"I understand that," said Nightingale.

The two women returned to the garden bearing a fruit cake and a jug of iced tea. Molly was also carrying two more cups. When they had sat down Nightingale turned to Laura and said: "I'm going to put a policeman on your door for the time being. We think this is a family feud going back a couple of hundred years. We have found out that Simon was part of the family that seem to be getting the rough end of it, and of course, now Matthew is a part of that family."

Laura looked alarmed. She had lost Simon and couldn't bear to think about losing Matthew.

"There's no need to get over-concerned, Mrs Goodall. But the policeman will go with him to school and back and stick by him whenever he goes out."

"Is that really necessary?" she asked.

"I think so, at the moment. The officer will be coming over to your house about 5.00 o'clock. I'm sure Matthew will feel very important, but it is necessary, I think."

"Well, I suppose so," said Laura. "And you're right, he will love it. He hasn't got over seeing me on television yet, and to have his own policeman will make him feel very important."

They ate their cake, which was delicious, and drank their tea. They passed an hour with Ralph and Laura sharing reminiscences of Simon. They laughed and cried and found that the conversation was a great help to Laura and Molly.

At last Nightingale and Keane had to take their leave and Laura had to collect Matthew from school. She had stopped meeting him now he was older, but had been doing it since Simon died. It gave both of them a feeling of security.

"Time to go home," said Nightingale and he and Keane drove back to the police station. Nightingale arranged for a good young officer to go to Laura's cottage, and then the two men took their leave from each other to go home.

"Don't forget Love Cats," said Nightingale as a parting shot.

"OK, guv. See you tomorrow."

They both drove home feeling a bit better about Laura and Matthew. Keane to ferret out The Cure and Nightingale to find the sonnet he needed and practice it. He had to go and see Nancy Dean the following day and ask her if she too wanted police protection. Tomorrow was another day and they both wondered what it would bring.

CHAPTER TEN

The next two days went by in a flash. Nightingale spoke to Nancy Dean about the danger they thought she was in, but she refused police protection. Nothing Nightingale could say persuaded her otherwise, so he could only respect her decision and warn her. The two policeman spent their time toiling through the family trees they had built up to double-check that there was nobody else in danger, which they satisfied themselves was correct. They only had to worry about Matthew Goodall and Nancy Dean. Matthew was as pleased as punch that he had police protection and loved every minute of it. It looked as if these two people were the last of their line. Nancy had no children and everybody hoped that Matthew would live to produce children when he grew up.

The day of Simon's funeral arrived, and Nightingale and Keane were at the church early. Ralph greeted them.

"Have you got your script, Richard?" he asked.

"Oh, yes," replied the policeman "It's a strange little sonnet, but I understand why the Goodalls had it read at their wedding. It's particularly pertinent for a funeral because it mentions in the last line about loving someone more after death. It will be my pleasure to read it. Will you announce it so I know when to stand up and come forward?"

"Oh yes," replied Ralph, "I'll let you know when we need you. Why don't you go and see Molly, I'm sure she can provide you with a coffee to while away half an hour?"

"That sounds lovely," said Keane, and the pair of them walked through the sunshine to the vicarage. Molly was very pleased to see them.

"Would you like orange coffee? It's one from the Mill."

"Yes, please," said both men together.

They sat in the garden under the tree. The coffee was delicious. They sat chatting to Molly until they saw the first mourners arrive.

"We'd better push off," said Nightingale and both men rose and made their way to the church. They sat half way back and kept their own counsel as people began to arrive. Soon the church was bursting at the seams with those who wanted to say goodbye to Simon. Nightingale thought that he must have been a very popular and much-loved member of the community.

The service was lovely. Ralph spoke abut Simon's childhood and teenage years, his meeting Laura and birth of Matthew. He announced Nightingale by saying: "We all know the unfortunate circumstances of Simon's death so early, and Detective Chief Inspector Nightingale who is investigating is here today and will read a sonnet by Elizabeth Barrett-Browning that Laura has chosen."

Nightingale went forward and explained that it had been read at Simon and Laura's wedding. He read it beautifully and many of the mourners were moved to tears. Simon was buried in the churchyard, and Nightingale and Keane stood a short way off.

"Look at the people," said Nightingale to Keane quietly. "We may find our murderer is here today. Anyone looking shifty, take a mental note of their description and I'll ask Ralph about them tomorrow."

"OK, guv," said Keane.

As the mourners moved off to go to a reception at the Lamb in Market Langley, Nightingale and Keane took their leave of Laura and returned to the police station. On the way, they swapped notes on the collected mourners.

"There was one man there that I didn't like the look of," said Keane. "He was looking at all the other people and seemed to be either looking for someone or doing what we were doing, you know, looking for the perpetrator."

"Describe him to me, Sherlock," replied Nightingale.

"He was about 5 foot 10 or thereabouts, aged about 40 to 45, receding hair which was brown (dyed I think), wearing grey flannels and a navy blue jacket. He looked at everybody round the grave as if he were committing them to memory."

"Was he indeed?" came the reply. Nightingale was most interested. "I'll talk to Ralph tomorrow and see if we can find out who he is. Well done, old chap, We'll make a policeman of you yet."

Keane laughed and said "I thought you read very well, sir. How did you learn the art of public speaking?"

"Don't you tell anyone, but when I was at school I was head boy and had to give numerous speeches. I sort of trained myself."

Here was something else Keane had learned about his boss. As he learned about the man he admired him more and more.

"Don't tell me you were a swat!" he laughed.

"Far from it. In those days you just had to be good at representing your school. I think I was appointed by rota. My father had been head boy in his day, you see."

"Well, however they got to pick you, well done, guv."

"Why, thank you, Keane, but not a word to anyone."

"OK, I'll keep mum," said Keane as they pulled into the station car park.

Nightingale said softly: "Oh, for goodness sake!"

The press were back. Not in such large numbers, but enough of them to cause a nuisance. They knew Nightingale now and surrounded the two policemen as they made their way into the station. They were calling out questions and thrusting microphones into the two men's faces. On the steps of the police station, Nightingale turned to face them.

"Gentlemen, if you would kindly shut up for a minute."

They stopped shouting and pushed their microphones forward.

"You know I can't discuss an on-going case. If we have any more news for you we will let you know, but at the moment there is nothing we can say, and you should know that. Thank you."

He turned and he and Keane entered the police station.

"What are we going to do about them?" asked Keane.

"I know, it's a pain isn't it? But that's what the modern world is coming to. 'It must be true because I read it in the paper.' That's how the vast majority of people think. We really can't tell them anything more, so they'll probably make it up. Come on, David, we've got to find the odd one out."

Keane didn't understand what Nightingale meant and so followed him to his office. Fisher was waiting for them.

"Hello, sir," said a surprised Nightingale. "Have you come to check up on us? We've been to Simon Goodall's funeral."

"I know, Richard. Did our friends from Fleet Street bother you?"

"Yes, they did!" said Nightingale strongly. "I don't think they will go away completely until we can announce the outcome of this case."

"No, and there really is nothing else we can tell them. I've had Cooper from Hendon on the phone. They are hounding them as well. They have made the connection. This is the biggest case they have got a scent of for years. If we just carry on and try to work round them, it's the best we can do." He smiled "So what's the next move?"

"Well, if we're right and this is a centuries-old feud, it stands to reason that we must have the perpetrator in our family tree somewhere. The Gough family seem to be killing off the Greene/Waters family. So we're going to find all the living members of the Gough family and see if we can find our killer. We'll have to investigate every one but I think it's the way forward."

"Well done, Richard. I'll let you get on with it. When you've got the names, let me know, and, er, have you got any biscuits?"

"Yes, sir," replied Keane. "We've got custard creams."

"Not one of my favourites. No Jammy Dodgers I suppose?"

"Sorry sir, no."

"Well, never mind, I'll just have to go without."

When Fisher had left the office. Nightingale and Keane looked at each other and burst into laughter.

"Well, he ought to buy his own biscuits!" said Nightingale

"Quite so, guv." Keane wondered if perhaps their biscuit fetish had spread round the station. He decided h would have to lock the biscuits in his drawer in future.

"Come on, David, let's get down to business." Nightingale took the complicated list of relatives on both sides of the mystery from his drawer and laid it on his desk.

The two men studied it for the best part of an hour.

"It's got to be somebody who moved from Hendon to Market Langley recently," said Nightingale.

"Or somebody who can travel between the two," countered Keane.

They came up with three names: Jessica Grover, Justin Cain and Steven Little. All people related to the Waters' way back who lived in Hendon. They found that the records had no examples of these three having any connection with Market Langley.

"I'll tell Cooper," said Nightingale, "He can look them up and report to us."

"Not another trip to Hendon, then?" asked a disappointed Keane.

"Not this time, old boy. I think Cooper can handle this part of the investigation. Now, put the kettle on and break out the custard creams while I phone Cooper."

Nightingale got through to Cooper.

"Hello, Ray, Richard Nightingale. Yes, we're all fine down here. Listen, I think we might need your help. We have traced three people in the Hendon area who may have some connection with the murders. We have been looking at family trees. It seems to us that someone from the Waters family might be our killer. If I give you the names could you find them and interview them?"

"Pleasure, Richard. You have been working hard, haven't you? Fire away and we'll see if we can round them up."

Nightingale gave Cooper all the information he needed, and the two policemen obviously enjoyed talking to each other. When the call was finished, Keane placed two cups of tea on Nightingale's desk and the now-opened custard creams.

"All we can do now is wait," said Keane.

"I think it's time to further my education David. I had the radio in the car playing this morning and heard a fabulous song by a group called The Doors. It was called Light my Fire."

"Oh yes, it's a very recent one. Everybody thinks it will be number one. They're an excellent rock group. Their lead singer is a chap called Jim Morrison. Would you like me to lend you their album on tape?"

"Yes please. You know I am really sorry that I've missed all this pop music. Of course, Clare knows them all. She's taken all her tapes out of the loft and we are working through them. Even though I have now found this music, my first love will always be classical music. Most of it doesn't assault the brain like a lot of the modern stuff does. Well I think it's time to go home. Perhaps Ray will ring us tomorrow. Are you ready to face the cameras again, Keane?

"Yes, guv. Come on, let's go."

The two men jostled their way out of the police station and into their cars. Now they were making headway. Neither of them could wait until the next day to see what Cooper had to tell them.

CHAPTER ELEVEN

Next morning Ray Cooper was at the police station early. Potter, his Sergeant, had found out the day before that Jessica Grover still lived in Hendon and worked in the public library. They knew they had to bring her in for questioning, but they were a bit concerned about the other two people. There was no sign of Justin Cain anywhere. He had paid Poll Tax until six weeks previously and had then just vanished. There was no sign of a forwarding address or anywhere he might live in Hendon. Steven Little was a fireman. Now he would have fitted the bill. They thought if they rounded him up first and then Jessica Grover, they could report the elusive Justin Cain to Nightingale when they had finished talking to their two suspects.

They went to the fire station and found that Steven Little was on duty. He was a large, robust man aged about 30 with a wife and two children, and the family lived in Hendon. They obviously could not take him away from his duties at that time, but Cooper said he would pick up the fireman at the end of his shift. Little understood that they would have questions for him. He had been as concerned about the murders in Hendon as anybody else and was only too pleased to help.

While they were waiting for the end of his shift, they went to the Library and found Jessica Grover. She was just finishing her early shift so they took her to the police station for questioning. Jessica had lived in Hendon all her life. She had an aging mother who lived there. She herself was slim and attractive, aged about 35, with dark hair that was pulled back to the nape of her neck. Potter seemed quite taken with her. Cooper chose to ignore this and they proceeded to take her to an interview room. Did she know anybody in Market Langley? No she didn't but she remembered the name of the town from the newspaper reports and her mother had mentioned a family that they were descended from in Hendon. She knew no names of the old family. They questioned her at some length. She seemed nervous and upset about being brought into the police station, which the two detectives thought was understandable. When they dropped the name Simon Goodall into the conversation she at once recognised it, again from the newspaper reports.

The two policemen tried to tell the difference between what she had gleaned from the newspapers and her own first-hand knowledge.

"Do you think your mother would talk to us about the family history?" asked Cooper.

"I'm sure she would," came the reply. "But can you possibly come to the house to talk to her? She'd be very upset if you brought her to the police station."

"Of course we can, Miss Grover," said Cooper. "Have you got to go back to work today?"

"No, it's my afternoon off today."

"Good, can we come to your house at about three o'clock this afternoon?"

"I'm sure that will be fine. Mum usually makes coconut cake on my early shift day and I'm sure she will cut you a slice."

"Yummy" said Potter, "Do you need us to take you home now or have you got a car at the Library?"

"No, I walk usually and the police station is on my way home. If you've finished with me I'd like to go and prepare Mum for your visit."

"Of course," replied Cooper. "Potter here will see you out and we'll catch up with you this afternoon."

When Potter returned to the office he had a grin on his face.

"What a charming woman," he said. "I don't think she's the one we're after, but it will be interesting to hear what the mother has to say about the old family."

"Yes, and coconut cake as well." Cooper looked at his watch. "Let's go to the canteen for a coffee and then we can go and collect Little."

These two policemen had not got Keane to make tea in the office nor to supply biscuits. If Cooper had known about the biscuit addicts from Market Langley perhaps he would have trained Potter in the same way. However, as it was they made their way to the Canteen and sat musing over Justin Cain.

"I think it's very suspicious that Cain went missing only weeks before Goodall was killed," said Potter.

"My thoughts exactly," replied Cooper "Let's steal a march on Nightingale and see what we can find out about Cain to present to Dickie when I ring him. We can do that after we have spoken to Little. Either of them could be our man." Cooper looked at his watch and finishing their tea they left to collect Little.

Steven Little was a charming man, obviously proud that he was a fireman and proud of his wife and family. He showed them photos of his family. He knew of Jessica Grover. She was a cousin of his, but he had never heard of Justin Cain so they thought the two men weren't closely related.

During the interview they discovered that he had never been to Market Langley, although he knew of it from the newspapers. Cooper cursed the press under his breath. Their job would be so much easier without them. Little was as puzzled as the policemen about the murders in Hendon. He didn't realise his family were so caught up in the whole situation. They took him back to the fire station to pick up his car, and left with the thought that they might need to speak to him again. They asked him not to leave Hendon without seeing them first.

"Oh, I'm not going anywhere," he said. "I know you've got to sort out these murders and thank you for not grilling me too hard."

"Not at all," said Potter. "We don't often get to speak to upright citizens in our line of work. Can you run 100 yards with a man on your back?"

"Yes, of course," replied Little "Do you want a demonstration?" and he bent down as if to pick up Potter.

"No, no, sir, it's quite all right" said Potter quickly and beat a hasty retreat. He wouldn't have liked to think what the rest of the fire station would say to see a fireman carrying a police sergeant on his back for 100 yards. As Potter went back to his car he turned to bid Little goodbye and saw that he had a grin on his face, very amused to see Potter leaving so quickly. Potter didn't know whether to tell Cooper about the incident, but finally decided not to, as the word would be all over the Nick in no time, and he didn't want that. He had been the culprit in making fun of his colleagues when they had done something that took some living down.

He drove back to the police station, and arrived in time to see Cooper up to his elbows in paper. Cooper had been printing all the information they had about Justin Cain, and there was a lot of it. He had minor form for possessing cannabis and being drunk and disorderly with cautions but not prosecutions, but both these matters had been some years ago. He had been clean since 1988 and stayed out of trouble, but they had very little information on the man himself, not knowing whether he was old or young as they didn't have a date of birth. Whoever had dealt with him had been very remiss on entering details on the computer, which Cooper put down to the fact that computers were complicated and very new to police work. He didn't understand them himself, and some of the more dyed-in-the-wool policemen still preferred to keep paperwork rather than try to use a computer. Cooper had heard that personal computers were the in thing, which would eventually make life easier, or so the blurb went, but he thought that it would be a few years before they had them installed at the police station.

Frustration set in for both policemen over the fact that they could not find what they wanted and eventually they gave up. They had missed their lunch and when they got to the canteen all that was left was a couple of salads. They settled for these and were delighted when the cook found them two pork pies to go with the salad.

"We'll go down to records after this and see if there is any information on Cain of the paperwork kind," said Cooper.

"Good idea. I bet there is. You can always rely on good old paperwork," mused Potter.

They ate their salads, which they found remarkably good.

"I'll have to have one of these again," said Cooper. "It's surprisingly nice."

"Good old Vera, finding those pork pies, they're just the ticket."

"Come on, sir, let's go and see Bulldog in records"

As they made their way to the old records office, Cooper mused: "What is Bulldog's real name? Do you know?"

"I don't think I ever did. He's always been Bulldog because he never lets go of a search until he's found something. He can just string information together."

"I suppose he'll be out of a job in a few years. Fingerprints are now on the computer, who knows what else will be possible."

"Except that computers rely on human input, and as we've seen with Cain, the information is not always there."

"I suppose so, but I don't think Bulldog will ever be out of work. He's got a brain like a computer himself."

The two men arrived at the record office and found Bulldog trying to find information about a woman who had been an habitual offender but had slipped out of their grasp.

"I don't know if she moved or died," he said to them.

"I've got another disappearing person for you," said Cooper. "Name is Justin Cain. He has previous for a couple of minor offences but never charged. Can you see if you've got anything. It will be back in the 70s, and if you've got any finger prints we would be eternally grateful."

"You know me. I'll find something," said Bulldog

"Can we leave you to it?" asked Cooper, "We've got an appointment to keep."

"Come back in a couple of hours and I'll let you know what I've found."

With a cheery goodbye Bulldog turned his attention to Justin Cain.

"If anyone can find him Bulldog will," said Potter. "Come on, sir, let's go and see Mrs Grover."

The two men made their way to the Grovers' address. It was a charming bungalow with a garden that was obviously loved and tended regularly. Jessica Grover came to the door and directed them to the back garden. A table was set up with the most delicious looking cake and plates with a selection of biscuits.

Mrs Grover was not what either of them expected. She was a very attractive woman in her early sixties. She wore jeans and a tee-shirt and had a stunning figure. She rose from her chair and offered her hand to Cooper.

"Brenda Grover," she said and Cooper shook her hand.

"DI Ray Cooper," he said, "and this is my sergeant, Chris Potter."

"How lovely to meet two real policemen. I haven't had many dealings with the police in my life, and I don't really know how I can help you today."

"We're interested in your family history," replied Potter. "I expect Jessica has told you that she is a descendant from a family with the name Gough."

"Yes, she did. There was a line of Gough family until about 80 years ago. I don't have all the information but my husband was related to them."

"We knew that the line went through your husband and not you. That's why we didn't know about you until Jessica told us. You are not a descendant like she is."

"No, I just married into the family."

Jessica appeared with a teapot in one hand and a sugar bowl in the other. Potter stepped forward to help her carry them. Brenda Grover indicated the cake on the table.

"Made today. Would you both like to try it?"

Both men said in unison, "Yes, please", and Jessica laughed. She cut two large slices and started to pour the tea. The policemen demolished their respective slices of cake.

"Absolutely delicious," said Cooper scooping up the last cake crumbs from his plate.

"Yes, gorgeous," agreed Potter.

Brenda Grover smiled. "Now," she said, "we lost the family name in about 1910. The last remaining Gough had no sons, just daughters, and the name became Grover from Katherine who married Fred Grover. Before that we go back to the landlord of the White Bear public house. He came from Sussex with his wife and settled here in the early 1800s."

"We know about the pub landlord. That's when the family first came to Hendon," said Cooper. "We are interested in any family members you might have knowledge of that we might not be able to find. People who have moved away or who live abroad. We have found Stephen Little and Justin Cain in Hendon, but we thought there might be more somewhere."

"Not that I know of," she replied. "We were always a small family and I don't think many, if any, of us moved away from Hendon." Then with a slight frown, "Why are you interested in the family?" she asked.

"I'm sure you know about the four murders in Hendon recently." She nodded. "Well, we have a theory that members of the Waters family are in danger from another family. We know you are related to the Gough side of the matter. And all the victims were related to another family called Waters. Do you know about them? All the victims were related, you see."

"How dreadful!" exclaimed Jessica.

"I can't tell you any more at this stage, but you have been very helpful. Your family is a small one and I don't think there are going to be any more of you. Our computer gave us Jessica and the two men, and we had hoped there would be more, but it looks as if it was right and there are no more."

The four of them sat in the garden long enough for the two men to have another slice of cake each and then they took their leave and made their way back to the police station.

"Great cake," said Potter.

"Yes, and what a turn up for the books. Great looking cook as well."

"Not at all what I was expecting," said Potter. "Lots of Mrs Robinson moments I'm afraid."

"Shame on you," laughed Cooper and the two men sat in amicable silence, each lost in his own thoughts until they arrived at the police station. Cooper immediately put a call through to Nightingale.

"Hello, Ray, I was wondering when I'd hear from you," smiled Nightingale.

Cooper told him everything they had learned during the day. Nightingale immediately jumped on the missing Justin Cain. He listened attentively to everything Cooper told him, making notes along the way.

"Thank you so much, Ray. I'll see what I can find out about Cain. Did Bulldog come up with anything?"

"Not yet, but you know him, he'll never give up. He'll find something if there is anything to find."

Nightingale hung up the phone after making his goodbyes. He had been busy as well. He had picked Neville Lambert's brain about untraceable poisons and had found that there were none that were completely untraceable. Of course if someone took a drug that was not prescribed for them there was always a danger of illness or even death, but again there would be traces of it in the body. Nightingale was stumped. How can you get someone to take a drug that was not prescribed to them and that left no trace? This was the only way his mind could go.

He was also concerned about the use of hydrocortisone cream that was not prescribed to any of the victims - and yet they had all applied it to their skin conditions. He would have to have a head-banging session with Keane the following day. Where was Keane? Nightingale hadn't seen him since lunchtime. He went on a tour of the building, and Keane was nowhere to be seen. Puzzled, Nightingale decided to go home. He would report to Reg Fisher tomorrow. Home seemed tempting, so he made his way along the lanes to his house. The trees were in full leaf now and the sun had gained strength with the passing time. Now it was really early summer. He pulled in to his driveway to be greeted by the cats.

"Mum not home yet?" he asked Bramble. The reply was much rubbing around his legs. "Come on, boys, let's see what I can find for you."

As he put his key into the door he felt a sense of peace, but how long would it last? He knew he had a lot to think about the next day.

CHAPTER TWELVE

Nightingale had not been able to visit the Saunders as he had hoped. When he got up the next day, he made a mental note to make the time to go and see them. He arrived at the police station just as Keane pulled into the car park.

"Morning, David."

"Morning, sir. What's on the menu today?"

As they walked to Nightingale's office, he asked:
"First of all, where did you get to yesterday? I looked for you in the late afternoon and you were nowhere to be found."

"I went to the library sir. I wanted to finally lay to rest the feeling that Ertol and Edward Gough perhaps were not the same person, but you're quite right, from the records there it seems that they are the same man. Isn't his history fascinating? And such a shame about his son. I also think we are right and that whoever our perpetrator is, is from Gough's family taking out the death of the son on Constance's family. I'm sure that our man thinks Patience set the fire that caused the boy's death in the caravan. Maybe the Gough connection have some form of grudge against all the descendants and you would be right, they must be a flower short of a bouquet."

"I think we are right, Keane, and I also have the best lead we have had so far." Nightingale told Keane about Justin Cain's disappearance from Hendon, and that Cooper's man Bulldog might have something today.

"See what you can find out about him. You might even have to check the social security records. If he's been working they should know where he is."

"There are all sorts of records that have started to be available on computers these days, sir. Leave it to me and I'll see what I can find."

"I must see Reg Fisher this morning. He's not up to speed on this latest lead. I'm quite excited about it, it's the best break we've had on this case,"

Keane made the tea and Nightingale quickly drank his cup and went to see Fisher. His parting short to Keane was a plea to rescue him in half an hour if he had not come back.

Fisher's office enfolded Nightingale like a wooden womb. The sun shone on the panelling and enclosed the two men in comfort. Fisher listened intently to what Nightingale had to say. He was equally as pleased with Cooper's work.

"How do you do it, Richard? You seem to be able to get the best work out of your colleagues wherever they are."

Nightingale smiled. "I don't know sir, but I think Cooper has done very well. I'll keep him in the loop of how this case goes along. Keane is looking for Justin Cain, and Bulldog is also working hard. When I've got anything else I'll keep you posted, of course."

"What are your plans today, Richard?"

"I'm going over old ground sir. Do you remember the case in '87 of the Saunders children?"

"Yes, every day of it," replied Fisher. "What a harrowing case that was. Are you going over it?"

"Not really. I thought I'd go and visit them. It's a good chance for me to think. I always seem to come up with ideas in a case when I'm doing something else."

"OK. I'll see you later and let's hope that Keane can find the elusive Cain."

Nightingale made his way back to his office and found that Keane had gone back to his office, presumably to telephone social services and begin his search. Nightingale's telephone rang. It was Cooper.

"Hello, Dickie, I thought I would tell you that Bulldog has found a set of fingerprints on the Justin Cain records. I've got Potter faxing them through to you now. I hope the image is good enough for you to compare them with those at the scene."
Nightingale nearly jumped into the air. He stood up.

"Good old Bulldog!" he exclaimed "I'll go and see if they've come through yet. What a star you turned out to be, Ray. I'll be in touch as soon as I have any information for you."

Nightingale made his way to the fax machine, and sure enough there was a fax from Cooper. He snatched it up and went to see the forensics team. They quickly were able to match the fingerprints to those on the wine bottles in Simon Goodall's house. Nightingale rushed to Keane's office.

"David, David, you'll never guess!"

Nightingale quickly told Keane his news. Keane was as excited as Nightingale.

"At last!" he said. "Now all I've got to do is to find Cain. I think this calls for the biscuits, don't you?"

"What have we got today?"

"Well, I took Fisher's advice and we've got Jammy Dodgers."

"Excellent! And to celebrate I'll make the tea, save you a job."

The two men polished off all the biscuits and both of them felt a sense of wellbeing. Now they really had something to work on.

Nightingale made his way to the car park, leaving Keane to try to find the elusive Justin Cain. He drove through the lanes feeling happier about the case now that they knew who the murderer was. It was just a case of finding him. The summer was now in early bloom and there was a display of wild flowers in the hedgerows. The journey to The Hall was a pleasant one. He reached West Downfold and turned into the driveway of the house. The last time he had been here was in 1987, and there had been fallen trees all the way along the wide sweep. Now there were tall rhododendrons in flower, and the few trees that were left were in full leaf. As he arrived at the house he saw the vet's van parked outside. The Saunders had a dog, Gerald, who must have been middle aged by now and he wondered what had brought on a house call.

The front door was open. He poked his head inside and called "Hello!" Sally Saunders appeared in the hallway. She started when she saw him and anxiously said: "Inspector. Is anything wrong?"

"No, no, Mrs Saunders. I thought I'd pay a visit to meet your young one. I hadn't seen you for so long and I thought it would be a good idea. I'm not disturbing you, am I?"

"No, not at all. Gerald is having an MOT. He's seven now and the vet thought it would be less stressful for him if she came here."

"Is that Nancy Dean?"

"Yes. Do you know her?"

"We have cats and we must use the same vet. How is she?"

"Come in and ask her, Inspector. Rosie is asleep at the moment, but you can be sure she'll wake up soon."

Nightingale entered the house, and as he made his way to the kitchen he said: "What a lovely name. I'll wait for her to wake up, if I'm not putting you out."

"Have a cup of tea with Robin and me. I'm sure Nancy and Sean would like one too."

The two of them entered the kitchen. Gerald was standing on the pine table, with Sean the nurse holding him gently, and Nancy was preparing a hypodermic needle. Both of them were surprised to see Nightingale, but both of them smiled at him.

"Hello, Inspector. How's Hops?" asked Nancy.

"He's fine. What are you going to do with that needle? I hope Gerald's not ill."

"No, he's remarkably well. This is just his annual vaccination. We thought we'd do it today while we were here. It's due next week, but we're killing two birds with one stone."

"I'll put the kettle on," said Robin, "Hello, Inspector, what brings you here today?"

"Just a social call to meet Rosie. I haven't seen her yet. I do love her name."

"Yes, she's Rosie May. We thought it was lovely too."

Nancy gave Gerald his injection in the scruff of his neck. He did not turn a hair.

"What a good boy!" said Sean. "You didn't feel that at all, did you?"

Gerald was placed back on the floor and went immediately to his basket in the corner.

"He knows me," said Nancy, "and I regret to say most of my patients don't like me. They know that I do things to them that they would rather I didn't. One of the unfortunate things about being a vet."

The kettle boiled and tea was made for everyone. Sally had wiped the table and they all sat round it.

"How are you, Nancy? I do wish you'd let me put a man on your door. You never know when you might need him."

"I'm fine, don't worry about me. I'm a big girl now and I'm sure I can cope with most things."

"Well, if you change your mind just ring me," said Nightingale, then to Robin and Sally: "It's a current case, we feel Nancy needs some looking after, but she won't have it."

"I know you can't discuss the case, but is it to do with the death of Simon Goodall?"

"You're quite right, I can't discuss it, but yes, it is that case."

"How exciting!" said Sally. She had recovered from the deaths of her children completely, and Nightingale was pleased to see she had gained some weight and her face was brighter than when he had last seen her. At that moment the child alarm on the work surface burst into life. Not with crying but with gurgling.

"Rosie's awake. I'll go and get her." Said Sally walking to the door. She soon returned with a delightful child in her arms.

Nightingale smiled, "How old is she now?" he asked.

"Two," replied Robin. "Going on 16!"

"I know what you mean" replied Nightingale. He extended his hand towards Rosie and she grabbed his fingers. Gerald left his basket and snuffled around Rosie's hanging feet.

"Gerald loves her," explained Robin. "It's a shame that he has to sleep in the kitchen or I'm sure he would sleep outside her door."

Nightingale remembered how Gerald had been devoted to Jenny and Martin, the two children who had been killed. In fact, he nearly lost his life trying to protect them at the time. That's when the Saunders moved the dog from sleeping outside the nursery to his bed in the kitchen.

Sally stood Rosie on the floor and she immediately threw her arms around Gerald's neck and hugged him.

"The feeling seems to be mutual," smiled Nightingale "But tell me, Sean. Do you still like Market Langley?"

"Love it," came the reply. "It's so different from Hemel Hempstead, and everybody is so friendly. You know, I don't think I'll ever leave."

"That's what I like to hear," said Nancy. "It looks as if we have you for the duration, then."

"I think so," Sean replied. "And I hate to hurry you, but you've got a surgery in half an hour."

Nancy looked at her watch.

"Come on then, Tonto, let's make tracks."

Robin walked Nancy and Sean to the door, then returned to the kitchen.

"Shall we take Rosie into the garden?" he asked. "It's lovely out there, and Sally could bring us some of her Victoria sponge cake – made this morning."

"What a lovely idea," came the reply. The garden was extensive, but there was a small area with children's toys scattered around it and four chairs. The four of them spent a lazy hour watching Rosie play and chattering about life in general. When Nightingale took his leave he went away feeling happier that the Saunders had made a new life for themselves with a new child - and what an adorable child. He drove back to the police station smiling. What would he find that Keane had discovered on his return? He could hardly wait to find out.

CHAPTER THIRTEEN

Nightingale and Keane had a head-banging session the next day. They had come to the conclusion that Justin Cain must be in his late 20s and that he must be supporting himself somehow, and therefore they assumed that he was working. Keane had traced him through the Social Security records up to eight weeks previously when he had just disappeared. They knew he was somewhere local to them as he had been at the scene of Simon Goodall's murder. The fingerprints on the wine bottles proved that.

"I still haven't spoken to Ralph Beddows about our man at the funeral," said Nightingale. "We know he's not Justin Cain because he's too old, but we must find out who he is."

"Where do we look for Cain now?" asked Keane.

"There's always a chance that he changed his name. He must know we are getting close to him. He must realise that he left his fingerprints at the scene. Either he is getting careless or he is taunting us."

"All killers think they are too clever to get caught. You taught me that," replied Keane. "I suppose that we looking for someone with access to drugs, legal or illegal. We must suppose that he brought the hydrocortisone cream with him and took it away when he left, and our mystery untraceable poison is something he must be able to lay his hands on."

"Quite right, Keane. Apparently there is no such thing as a poison that is completely untraceable. There are those that work with a delayed action, but there is always a trace of them left. I think we are looking at something that is a legal drug given to someone who doesn't need it, resulting in death."

"But how does he make his victim take it? Most people would not take something not knowing what it would do to them. Well, any sensible person anyway."

"He must put it in something, like the wine. Hang on a minute, I've just had a tremendous brain wave. All the victims had eczema, I think we should guess that it is hereditary in the family and all of them had applied hydrocortisone cream. What do you think? Is the drug in the cream? That gives us a reason why he took it away with him."

"Brilliant, sir! But what would disappear without a trace?"

"I don't know, but Neville may be able to help us. I'll ring Ralph Beddows about the man at the funeral and then I'll put a call through to Neville. Come on Keane, let's get to it."

Keane was amazed at Nightingale's train of thought. He just might be on to the truth of the matter. He realised that he would not get promotion to Inspector until he could think like Nightingale. He knew that Nightingale was a particularly cerebral man whom he admired tremendously. He also knew that while he was learning from him he was getting the best training possible.

Nightingale rang the vicarage. Ralph Beddows answered the phone.

"Morning, Richard, how are you?"

"I'm fine, and very pleased to tell you that we are making progress. How is Laura Goodall?"

"She OK. Learning to live without Simon, and Matthew still doesn't fully understand what's happened, but he has made a good friend in his policeman, and thinks it's great to have police protection."

"Let's hope it won't be for long."

"What can I do for you, Richard? I don't suppose you rang me to ask about the Goodalls."

"Quite right. Do you remember a man at Simon's funeral who looked a bit shifty? He is about 40 with little hair, about 5ft 10?"

"Yes, I do, but you don't have to worry about him. He was from Hendon CID."

"And nobody told me? I'll have a few words about that. How do you know this?"

"He told me, showed me his warrant card, so I know he's kosher."

"Thanks, Ralph. Hope to see you soon, but I'm sure you understand, I'm a bit busy at the moment. Give Molly my best wishes."

"Will do. Yes, when all this is over, we'll get together. Bye, Richard."

Nightingale bade Ralph goodbye and immediately phoned Ray Cooper in Hendon.

Cooper had not told him of their representative at the funeral for fear of upsetting him. He did not bank on Keane's excellent observation, but he apologized to Nightingale and told him that their man had not found out anything that Nightingale did not already know. Nightingale was mellow with Cooper, but made sure that he knew what Nightingale thought of this deception. He hung up, still friends with Cooper but with both men holding each other in greater respect.

Nightingale turned to Keane.

"You heard that. I think Ray overstepped his authority and he knows how I feel about it, but 10 out of 10 for observation David."

"He can't bear to think we might solve the murders where he failed. Put it out of your mind sir, you have a good relationship with Cooper. Don't let this spoil it."

"Yes, you're right, I'll try to forget it." Then mentally shaking himself he phoned Neville Lambert. Neville had just finished a post mortem and came to the phone. The two men greeted each other with mutual affection.

"I want to pick your brains again," said Nightingale.

"What can I do for you? What's entered your head now?"

"Is there a drug, legally obtained, that, when given to a person who doesn't need it, could kill them?"

"I'm sure there are a few, but I take it we are talking about a drug that disperses quickly. Is our killer a doctor then? Ordinary folk wouldn't be able to get their hands on a drug not intended for them."

"I'm sure it's someone in the health professions in some way. What do you think, Neville, is it possible?"

"The first thing that springs to mind is warfarin, used - as I'm sure you know - for heart conditions, but I'm sure it would show up and the condition of the victim's blood after death would be an indicator. Our victims had no adverse toxicology results."

"Is that the only one you can think of?"

"Well, there is always good old insulin. The reason patients take it so often is that it disperses in the body very quickly and leaves no trace."

Nightingale was all attention.

"Well, I didn't know that. So if our killer could get the insulin into the victims when they didn't need it, it would kill them?"

"Yes, indeed. Diabetics who need it are monitored very carefully. It's potentially a lethal drug."

"One more question, Neville. Could it be put into a tube of hydrocortisone cream?"

"I've never thought of that one, Richard. I suppose it could be, but you could only use the cream once shortly after putting the Insulin in it. It would be gone within a few hours. What a clever person our killer is, and how clever you are to think of it. I suppose that's why the killer took the cream away with him when he left the scene."

"That's what we think. Now keep mum about this until we find our killer. If the press get hold of it, our killer will know we're on to him and go to ground."

"Sure thing, old chap. Glad I could help. Insulin, eh? What a turn up for the books."

The two men finished their conversation and Keane broke into an enormous grin.

"Insulin! You are clever, guv. Do we tell Fisher?"

"Not yet Keane. I think your next job is finding out from the local doctors who on their list is an insulin-dependent diabetic. It shouldn't take too long, there are only two doctors in the area. Can you ring them today?"

"Yes, guv. I don't suppose there are many diabetics who take insulin around here, I'll give it my best shot. What are you going to do?"

"I'm going to pay a visit to Laura Goodall and Matthew. It's about time I brought them up to date, but no mention of insulin I think."

"Off you go, then. I seem to be surgically attached to the telephone at the moment. I'll bring you up to date later."

Nightingale drove out to West Downfold listening to The Doors tape that Keane had lent him. He particularly appreciated 'Riders on the Storm'. He nearly stopped the car to listen to it. He had never heard anything like it and played it twice.

He arrived at Laura Goodall's house with his head filled with the song. He shook his head and made his way to the front door. Laura was pleased to see him and listened intently to the information he gave her. He made no mention of Justin Cain or of insulin. He wanted to keep those two things under his hat.

"How is Matthew getting along?" asked the policeman.

"Oh, he loves his protection officer, they are very good friends now. He is always sad to see him go off duty when the uniformed man comes to stand outside at night. He's beginning to realise that all the attention is because of his father's death and he's slowly coming to the realisation that he will not see Simon again. I think he is old enough to remember his father in years to come, thank goodness.

"I never did really thank you for reading the sonnet at the funeral. You made a very good job of it. It's lovely isn't it?"

"I knew bits of it from my days at school but not all of it. Yes, it's lovely."

"I've made a rhubarb crumble for dessert tonight. I'm sure Matthew won't mind if I let you try it. He'll be sorry he missed you but I'm so glad he has school to keep him occupied."

"I'd love some, Mrs Goodall. Thank you very much."

He sat at the kitchen table eating the crumble, which was delicious and wondered about Laura Goodall. She seemed so composed but her eyes were red from crying. He supposed that she did her crying when Matthew was at school. She had filled the house on every flat surface with pictures of Simon taken over the years. With Matthew when he was younger and the three of them together. She obviously wanted to remember him before this tragedy happened and to keep him in Matthew's memory.

Nightingale finished his dish of crumble and offered to wash it up.

"Thank you for offering, but there's no need. That's what dishwashers are for," she replied.

"My wife is trying to convince me to buy a dishwasher. I suppose I'll have to give in, but we don't have enough dishes to fill one."

"You don't have to buy a full-size one, you can get three quarter and half sizes."

"I didn't know that. I think I'll take her to the shops this weekend."

Both of them were trying to get the tragedy off their minds, Laura because the memory was so painful and Nightingale because he didn't want to upset her any longer. They chatted about the benefits of kitchen appliances for another ten minutes and Nightingale took his leave of her.

"What a brave woman," he thought as he walked to his car. "She must be so glad that she had Matthew as a little piece of Simon left on earth."

When he got back to the police station he found Keane surrounded by sheets of paper.

"What's all this, Keane. Surely there aren't that many diabetics in the area."

"No sir, there aren't, but I've got a list of diabetics who do not take insulin as well"

"Why?"

"Because it was pointed out to me by Dr Morton that someone who is not insulin-dependant may say they are to a strange doctor to obtain a prescription for it."

"Good thinking, Dr Morton," smiled Nightingale, "but I think we'll start with those who have insulin. We only need the men and somebody who moved here recently."

"Good idea, guv. Shall I put the kettle on?"

"Oh yes please" replied Nightingale, "Have we got any biscuits?"

"Yes, guv. Crumble Creams."

"I don't think I've had those before, but I'm sure they will be delicious. This afternoon we'll run the diabetics through the police computer to see if we can find anyone with form."

The tea was soon made, and much to his surprise Nightingale finished off most of the biscuits in no time.

"We must have those again, Keane. They make a lot of crumbs but they are yummy."

"I thought you'd like them," replied Keane, "so I bought two packets." And he produced another packet from the drawer, Both men laughed. It was a moment's escape from the terrible job that they had to do. That afternoon they would start on their monumental task. Nightingale did not think it would lead anywhere, but it had to be done. They would find Justin Cain eventually, maybe not today, but find him they would.

CHAPTER FOURTEEN

Nightingale left Keane to carry out his task and went to Fisher's office. The Superintendent was at his desk. He motioned Nightingale to sit down and looking up from his paperwork, said: "What have you got for me Richard? Good news, I hope."

Nightingale quickly told him about Justin Cain and their search amongst the diabetics in the area.

"I think Cain's too clever to be registered with a doctor, but if he isn't he must be in the medical area somewhere. I'm going to contact the hospital this afternoon to see if they have any new employees that would fit the bill. Cain can't just have disappeared, and we think he must be working - but if he's changed his name he could be anywhere. I think our trawl of medical professionals is our best bet. I will find him, Reg, I know I will, but I've got to do it before he claims another victim. If I were him I'd be after Nancy Dean, she refused police protection and she's wide open."

"We can't make her accept our protection, you know. Does she know the full extent of the danger she's in?"

"I don't think so, Reg. I've tried to tell her, but she thinks she can look after herself."

"OK, Richard, I won't stop you working, but keep me posted. I know you will find him eventually, let's hope it's in time."

Nightingale returned to Keane's office. "Poor David," he thought, "He's got an almost impossible task."

Keane looked up and grimaced.

"Do you think computers will ever work faster?" he said. "This one takes an age before it does anything useful."

"One day perhaps, but we've got to make the best of what we've got. Come on let's have some lunch and leave it chuntering."

"OK, what a welcome relief. I hope they've got something good on the menu today."

The two men ate their lunch in silence, then suddenly Nightingale said: "Of course he doesn't have to be a health professional. He could be a hospital porter or somesuch. When I talk to the hospital people this afternoon I'll see if they have any new employees in every field. What other health-related professions are there, Keane?"

"Well, there are care homes and clinics. We have a couple of retirement homes in the area and we have St Agatha's Clinic."

"Yes, of course we do. I'll get on to them as well. Good old David, between us we will crack this case."

They finished their meal with a doubtful egg custard tart and returned to Nightingale's office. They looked up the telephone numbers of the care homes and St Agatha's, and Keane went to the computer room to see if it had found anyone that may have been Cain. There were no new patients registered with either of the doctors and there wasn't even a parking ticket between the established patients. Keane sighed and thought that he would have been peeved if he had to do all that work without the computer. It would have taken days. He needed time to think. He decided to go for a walk to the town pond. It was peaceful there with only the herring gulls for company. He took a new notebook and made his way out of the police station.

Nightingale meanwhile was busy on the phone to Sunny Mount, the second of the care homes. All their staff were female and there were no new faces over the past couple of months. Nightingale reluctantly phoned St Agatha's.

"Yes, we have a new theatre technician," he was told. "He started here two months ago. If you can give us half an hour, we'll dig up his record and references."

"What's his name?" asked Nightingale.

"Sean Adamson," replied the woman on the other end of the phone. Nightingale sprang out of his seat. "I'll be there in half an hour."

He rushed to Keane's office only to find him on his way down the stairs.

"Where are you going?" he asked. Keane told him. "There's no time for that. I've found someone at St Agatha's who is a very good bet. His name is Adamson."

Keane looked at him blankly.

"Don't you see? Did you never go to Sunday School? Cain was the son of Adam and Eve. He murdered his brother. So it looks as if has changed his name from Cain to Adamson. Adam's son."

"What a clever thing," replied Keane.

"Oh, he is clever," answered Nightingale "We've got to be there in half an hour."

"It'll take us that long to get there and park. What are we waiting for?"

The policemen drove to At Agatha's with controlled excitement. It was an imposing building put up two hundred years ago, with impressive windows and a very grand entrance. Nightingale and Keane were taken to the Human Resources office where they met Amy, who looked after staff records. Adamson had gone to them with excellent references from a private hospital in Hemel Hempstead.

"Where's that?" asked Keane.

"Not a million miles from Hendon," replied the senior officer. "We know someone else who came from Hemel Hempstead."

"I don't. Who have you got in mind?"

"Do you remember when Clare and I took Hops to the vet? The new head nurse is called Sean, and he spent ten minutes telling us all about Hemel Hempstead where he used to live."

"Do you know his surname?"

"No, I didn't ask him, but I'll bet it's the same man. Do you have a picture of him?" he asked Amy.

"All our staff wear ID badges with a picture on them. I think I've got a copy of it here."

Both men looked at the photograph. Nightingale's face broke into a broad smile. "That's him" he said, "but how can he work at the vet's and here?"

"He works here on Mondays and Thursdays," they were told.

"Have you got a home address for him?"

"Of course. 21 Barnard's Way, Market Langley."

"Come on, Keane, there's no time like the present! Thank you, Amy, you've just solved our case."

The two men drove out of the clinic.

"Now, the question is, where will we find him? It's Wednesday today so he will probably be at the vet's. We'll go there first."

They pulled into the vet's car park. The surgery van was parked there. They went inside and found Nancy Dean behind the reception desk.

"Hello Inspector. To what do we owe this pleasure?"

"Is Sean here?" asked Nightingale

"Yes, he's in the cat ward getting a patient ready for surgery. A simple spay operation."

"Can we go down there?"

"Yes. What's this all about?"

Neither of them answered her. She led them to the cat ward and they found Sean gently tending to Bella, the cat in question.

"Well, Inspector," he said. "I guessed you'd catch up with me eventually, but I have to say you've been quicker than I thought. Nancy was to be the Waters for tonight, but you got to me too early."

"Come on Sean. You're nicked," said Keane and took a pair of handcuffs out of his jacket.

As they passed Nancy she looked at Nightingale with anguish.

"Do you mean, Sean, that you were going to kill me tonight?"

"Oh yes, Nancy," came the reply. "Veterinary insulin works better than human insulin. I told you I had something for your eczema."

One of the nurses came to comfort Nancy, who was looking very shocked.

"See she's OK," said Keane to the nurse and they put Sean into the car. Keane sat with him in the back and Nightingale drove them back to the police station.

Once in an interview room, Sean was only too ready to tell them how clever he was. Neville Lambert had been right. The hydrocortisone cream had been obtained from St Agatha's, and the insulin was the veterinary variety. He had injected an amount into the top of the tube of cream so that when the victim put it onto his or her eczema it quickly caused their demise. As to why he was doing it, the answer to that went back to Constance and the child she gave to Ertol.

"You see, Edward was my brother. He didn't have a mother and his father's family was all he had. He was only 12 when Patience burned him to death."

'We don't know that for sure," said Keane.

"I do," came the reply. "They buried him on the north side of the church too. Nobody goes there. It's cold and dark and Edward deserved to be in the sun. His father made a new life for himself and had a new family. Nobody remembered Edward."

"I'm sure his father did," said Nightingale.

"I really thought you wouldn't find me," said Cain. "What was it that gave me away?"

"A man called Bulldog," answered Nightingale, and he related the incident from when Cain was a teenager.

"Bloody hell!" came the reply, "All those years ago. You must admit, Inspector I really had you foxed, didn't I?"

"Are you a veterinary nurse or a theatre technician by training?" asked Keane "Which of them is it?"

"I trained as a vet nurse when I was in my late teens. It takes three years, you know. Then I trained as a theatre nurse. I lied about being a registered nurse when I first went to a hospital. It's just the same as veterinary nursing, just a different anatomy."

Nightingale watched Cain's face as he told them the story. He was full of his own importance and was sure that nobody had ever been as clever as him. They put him in a cell and Keane typed up his confession.

"Well done, guv," he said.

"I knew we'd get him eventually, but I'm so glad we did it before he'd killed Nancy. I'll go and see Fisher while you do that. You know this man is evil. I don't think he is mentally ill, he's been too clever. I think he firmly believes that he was doing the right thing to revenge his family. We have a lot of people to tell about this. I expect Fisher will call a press conference. Oh Keane, thank goodness it's over."

Nightingale walked along the corridor to Fisher's office feeling as if he had lost the weight that was pushing him down. He smiled as he knocked on the door and entered when he heard the cheery "Come in."

Printed in Great Britain
by Amazon.co.uk, Ltd.,
Marston Gate.